"What I'm thinking sounds crazy."

Triss stared into Hunter's eyes with conviction, as if willing him to believe what she was about to say.

He already did. He might still be rankled by how suddenly she'd dropped out of his life—out of his kids' lives—but that didn't change what he knew about her: She was intuitive, sharp and levelheaded. She was not prone to drama, exaggeration or misinterpretation. And if Triss Everett had something bizarre to say, she'd say it only if she knew it to be true.

"I can handle crazy."

Her eyes were dark, troubled in a way he'd never seen before. "I don't think what happened was an accident, Hunter," she said finally. "I think someone caused the fire. I think someone hoped I would die. And I think that same person may have killed before. At Harmony."

That, he hadn't expected. Hunter reached for what to ask next, and Triss narrowed her eyes.

"You said you could handle crazy."

Sara K. Parker has been a writer ever since she was gifted a 4x6 pin-striped journal for her tenth birthday. Her writing hobby has since grown into her dream career—writing for Love Inspired, freelancing for magazines and teaching English at a community college. She and her husband live in northwest Houston with their four children, two—soon to be three!—mischievous dogs and an extremely vocal senior cat.

Books by Sara K. Parker

Love Inspired Suspense

Undercurrent
Dying to Remember
Shattered Trust
Security Measures

SECURITY MEASURES

SARA K. PARKER

HARLEQUIN® LOVE INSPIRED® SUSPENSE

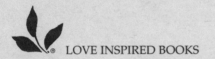

LOVE INSPIRED BOOKS

ISBN-13: 978-1-335-23229-8

Security Measures

www.Harlequin.com

Printed in U.S.A.

He revealeth the deep and secret things: he knoweth what is in the darkness, and the light dwelleth with him.
–Daniel 2:22

To Erica, Julie and Megan.

God knew I wouldn't do well in Texas without my three sisters, so He gave me you. Thank you for doing life with me—whether we're laughing until we cry or crying until we can laugh again. Friendship with each of you has shaped me, grown me, blessed me.

ONE

Gravestones lined both sides of the cobblestone path and dotted the acreage beyond. The cemetery was a patchwork of narrow footpaths, ancient trees and wrought-iron garden benches. Wind chimes hung from tree branches, their sorrowful melodies echoing through the graveyard. A couple of months ago, Triss Everett might have found the place charming, even beautiful. Today, after attending a funeral for the fourth time in three weeks, she couldn't escape soon enough. Her black boots crunched through piles of autumn leaves, the wind whipping her long black hair as more foliage swirled from the wooded canopy. Unfamiliar heat stung her eyes, tears threatening as the cemetery blurred around her.

She sucked in a sharp breath of chilly air and focused on the parking lot ahead. She'd learned after the first funeral to park in the overflow lot. No one parked there, and she could avoid the dreaded lingering that happened after the burial—the hugs and tears and words that could do nothing to ease anyone's suffering.

Maybe she should have expected this when she'd signed a twelve-month graduate-student housing contract with the Harmony Senior Living Community in August. But she hadn't. And she certainly hadn't expected to forge friendships with the residents. Warm, deep, meaningful friendships. She'd spent years pouring her energy into work and school, too busy and driven to invest in friendship. But the pace was slower at Harmony, where she and four other graduate students had embarked on a pilot program in which they received room and board in exchange for volunteer hours and companionship with the residents. There, friendships had formed as she spent her contracted volunteer hours partaking in chair fitness, bingo and weekly outings with the residents. Soon, she'd found herself taking on extra hours to sit with her new friends at hair appointments, mealtimes and dialysis sessions. She couldn't help but care about them as she grew to know their personalities and histories, their hobbies and families.

A tear escaped and she swiped it away, hurting. Angry. If she had known she'd get so attached, she never would have signed the agreement.

Her little black Mustang sat alone at the edge of the lot, and she hurried to it, determined to get a handle on her emotions. It had been nearly six years since she'd let herself cry. All other pain had paled in comparison to that cold November day, until now. Forcing away the tears, she unlocked her car and climbed into the driver's seat. She turned the key in the ignition and glanced in the rearview, her hand on the gearshift. But her gaze caught on her reflection, the pallor of her face, the glaze of tears in her eyes, and an ache rose in her chest. She squeezed her eyes shut, tears leaking as her shoulders began to heave, and a keening sound rolled from her throat—raw grief that could not be contained. The memory forced its way into her heart until she finally gave in to the weight of loss, her forehead coming to the steering wheel as she grieved for her four unlikely friends and their loved ones, and also for the life she'd turned her back on years ago.

She stayed like that for long minutes until she'd poured out what felt like a lifetime of guarded emotion. Then she cleared her throat and pulled a couple of napkins from the console, blowing her nose and drying her cheeks. No mascara to worry about since she seldom wore makeup. Glancing at the clock, she put the car in Reverse. She needed to get moving. She'd volunteered to help set up the reception at Harmony, and guests would be arriving soon.

Forcing herself into business mode, she drove away from the cemetery and pulled onto the highway. But even as her tears dried, the ache in her chest tightened, grief giving way to anxiety. Four deaths in three weeks, but she had nothing she could report to police.

No one else even suspected a problem. On the contrary, her fellow grad-student friends and Harmony staff she'd come to know had all gently assured her that it was normal to want to place blame when grieving. They'd pointed out other truths as well: that her security background made her more paranoid than she needed to be, that all four of the residents had had underlying health conditions and that "old people die."

That last gem had been contributed by Riley Jasper, the youngest of the grad students and the most immature. Some kind of genius, she'd started college at fifteen, and now, at nineteen, her social tact was still sorely lacking. Not that Triss was one to judge. She was well aware that her own personality was considered by most to be cold at best, abrasive at worst.

But that was beside the point. Riley Jasper's comment, genius notwithstanding, was ignorant. The four dead residents had not been that old, and all had passed swiftly, without warning.

Even the Harmony staff agreed that four deaths in such a short period was unusual in the forty-eight-bed community—though not unheard of. But Triss had to admit that her suspicions were a little far-fetched. Could someone in the home really be set on murder? Or was it simply a difficult season of loss?

Whatever the cause, and regardless of the skepticism of her new friends, Triss figured that tightening security at Harmony wouldn't hurt anyone. She'd worked as a security agent for Shield Protection Services for a little over two years, and the four deaths at Harmony had not only piqued her suspicions but had also alerted her to the lax security around the community. Two days ago, she'd proposed some simple ideas to boost security. No one had taken her seriously, but Triss was never one to go down without a fight, and—

A loud pop sounded behind her and she jolted, glancing in the rearview. Had a rock hit her rear window? She didn't see a crack, thankfully. The car had already been in the shop a few times this year, and Triss didn't have extra cash for more repairs. Not seeing anything, she started to return to her thoughts when she picked up an acrid, burning scent.

Again, she checked the rearview. This time, her heart lurched. Smoke! A thick, black cloud plumed from the rear of her vehicle.

She didn't think, just reacted, checking her mirrors as she swerved toward the shoulder. Smoke billowed above her gas tank in black waves. She didn't have much time. A driver laid on his horn as Triss nearly plowed into the side of his truck and swerved again, overcompensating with the wheel. Her tires spun, the car flying across the highway and out of her control as she pumped the brakes and tried to get it under control. Tires screeched and horns blared as her Mustang skidded sideways into a speed-limit sign, the impact sending her car into a spin, and then she was sliding over the shoulder and into a shallow embankment.

In a daze, Triss reached for her seat belt, her hands shaking as she jerked it off and grabbed the door handle. The door wouldn't budge! She jabbed at her window control, but it didn't respond. Smoke started to fill the car, burning her throat and lungs as she looked in terror at a bright orange flame too close to the gas tank. Desperate, she yanked at the handle again, a painful cough taking hold and stealing her strength even as she frantically scanned her car for something she could use to break a window. She wished she'd brought her gun, but she never carried it off duty.

Dread grew as thick as the smoke inside the car. Her breathing was labored and punctuated by coughs, and her hazy mind drifted back to the cemetery she'd just come from, the red and gold leaves flitting to the ground. Searching through her console, she fought rising panic as the car grew hotter, the smoke thickening. Desperate, she yanked at the door again, knowing it was futile. Cars pulled over ahead, shadowy figures running toward her, but the smoke was thick, stealing her air, and she was sure they were too late.

Hunter Knox threw his truck into Park and ran to the back, rummaging through his supplies for his window breaker, and then sprinted to Triss's Mustang. A crowd had gathered, a couple of people using various tools to try to break open windows, while others warned the crowd to stand back. A small flame was licking up the back of the car, an explosion imminent. Black smoke filled the interior.

"Move aside!" Hunter yelled, forcing his way through the crowd to the front of the car. Deciding his best option was the front windshield, he climbed up on the hood and kneeled as he locked eyes with Triss. The fear there pierced his heart as smoke swirled behind her. He'd known Triss for two years and had never seen her scared. "Cover your face!" he yelled, and placed the tool in the center of the passenger side of the windshield. The glass cracked immediately, and he pushed the rest of it in, others joining in to clear the shards as Triss attempted to pull herself up and out of the car.

She was weak, gasping for air. Hunter reached down, clearing the glass. "Try to stand!" He wanted to scream for her to hurry, to focus. He was afraid he'd lose her to an explosion at the last moment, but she was dazed, attempting to find her footing on the seat to push her way out.

Leaning close, Hunter held out his arms to her. "Hold on to me!"

She reached toward him, her hands locking on his upper arms as he latched onto her and yanked her over the dash and through the broken window. Others, eager to help, brought her to the ground as Hunter jumped off the hood. Easily lifting her into his arms, he again warned the crowd to retreat and jogged away from the burning vehicle.

Triss's hand clutched the front of his shirt, her head tucked under his chin as he moved toward his truck. He'd only taken a few dozen steps when an explosion erupted behind them. Triss jerked in his arms, and he tightened his hold, glancing back to see her car in flames, bystanders gawking and filming.

A shudder ran through him as he considered what would have happened if he had simply finished up his shift and gone home today. Shaken, he walked to the passenger side of his truck and shifted Triss so he could open the door.

"You can put me down," she said, the words whispered at the base of his neck, her voice raspy. "I can stand."

He was surprised she hadn't wriggled out of his arms already. She was the most fiercely independent person he'd ever met. But he suspected that if he set her on her feet right now, she'd collapse.

"I've got you."

She didn't argue, her fingers still grasping his shirt, her silky black hair grazing his chin. He pulled the door open, easily seating her inside and adjusting the seat so she could lean back. She'd started shivering, whether from shock or the chill in the air, he couldn't be sure. But the truck was still running, and he leaned over to turn the heat on full-blast. He yanked off his jacket and tucked it gently under her chin and around her arms and sides.

She stared up at him, eyes so dark he could barely make out her pupils, long lashes shielding her thoughts. They'd been coworkers for a long time, and he was used to her quiet, but this was different.

"Are you hurt anywhere?"

She shook her head. "I don't think so."

"Good. Just hang tight for a couple of minutes." He pressed her door shut and reached for his phone to call for help, but he could already hear sirens. Plenty of others had likely already called in the accident.

Assuming it had been an accident.

He eyed her flaming car as he moved to the driver's side of his truck. He didn't know a lot about cars, but he was pretty sure it was rare for a vehicle to start smoking near the gas tank and then explode. As far as he knew, fires usually started under the hood.

He frowned, sliding into his seat and closing his door. Or maybe he'd been working at Shield too long. Nearly five years in, he had to admit he was prone to suspicion. It wasn't like she'd been driving a brand-new vehicle. The Mustang had to be at least ten years old. There must have been a problem with it because the alternative was that someone had caused the fire, and that didn't seem likely. Who would want to harm Triss? What motive could someone have?

Not that he and Triss spent much time talking about her personal life. In fact, he'd barely seen her since she'd moved into Harmony nearly four months ago. She'd cut her hours at Shield and switched to the night shift three days a week, so they only worked together on the rare occasion one of them took on a double. She'd explained that the free room and board would help her finish her graduate degree faster, which he respected. She had her sights on a career as a forensic investigator with the FBI, and he had no doubt she'd be one of the best in the field. But he suspected she'd had other motives for cutting her hours at Shield—motives that included avoiding Hunter and his two kids. He couldn't blame her for that, even if he wished things could be different. She had big goals, and an instant family would only slow her down.

Next to him, she had tugged his jacket closer and closed her eyes.

Something had shifted between them over the past year or so, their friendship growing rapidly. In fact, not long ago, Hunter had gotten the impression that they might have something deeper than friendship, but Triss had backed away every time he'd started to get too close. Still, despite the growing distance between them, Hunter had been compelled to go to the cemetery a while ago. He'd been late because he'd been waiting for his relief at work, but was just in time to see her running from the graveside, her normally deep tan skin pale. He'd stopped his pursuit when she climbed into her car, slammed the door shut and leaned her forehead on her steering wheel, her shoulders quaking with grief. He had never seen Triss emotional, and he had a feeling she didn't want him to. Instead, he'd gotten in his truck and decided to follow her at a distance to make sure she got safely to Harmony, considering her emotional state.

Turned out, she hadn't been safe at all.

He glanced over at her again, noting that her shaking was starting to subside. She was still silent, her eyes closed, her shiny black hair spilling over her shoulders and onto the reclined seat.

For a moment, he thought she'd fallen asleep, but then she opened her eyes and turned her head toward him.

"Why are you here?"

The blunt question caught him off guard, but it was Triss's way.

"I heard—"

"I mean—"

They both spoke at the same time, and Hunter stopped, waiting.

"I mean, you usually work day shift," Triss explained. "Shouldn't you still be there?"

"I heard Luke talking with Roman yesterday about the funeral. I thought you could use a friend."

Triss's brother Luke had been friends with their boss, Roman, for years, but beyond the daily prayer meeting they held each morning, the two rarely had personal conversations on the job—which was why Hunter had taken note of yesterday's conversation, even though he knew he shouldn't be eavesdropping.

In fact, he'd almost talked himself out of going to the cemetery today. He didn't know the man who had died, and he hadn't even seen Triss in weeks. But he'd wanted to be there for her. As far as he could tell, she didn't have many good friends—if any—and he knew what it was like to navigate death alone. He wouldn't wish it on anyone. Especially Triss, who he had long suspected had already endured her fair share of sorrow.

She looked away, and he wondered what she was thinking. Triss was a difficult person to read, even more difficult to get to know. Normally, he would steer clear of someone with her personality. But the day she'd offered to watch his kids when their nanny was sick had changed everything. He'd come home to peals of laughter, walking into a mess in the kitchen that resembled the aftermath of an indoor blizzard. Powdered sugar and flour covered nearly every surface, the kids and Triss included. His kids were rolling with giggles, and Triss was leaning against the counter, helpless against the laughter.

Until that moment, he wasn't sure Triss even knew how to laugh, how to really smile. And since then, he'd made it a mission to hear that laugh and see that smile as often as he could. Which hadn't been often since August.

He turned fully to her, but she didn't look at him, her profile tilted toward the window.

"Must have been a quick funeral at the church," Hunter said. "I barely made it to the cemetery before you were flying out of the parking lot." She was teased mercilessly at Shield for her lead foot. Usually, she laughed it off. Now, she adjusted her position in the seat, turning toward her mangled car.

"Yes. The service was short and sweet." She stared out the rear window, then finally looked at Hunter. "So, you followed me out?"

He read the question in her gaze, but didn't think she'd appreciate that he'd seen her crying and had worried about her. "Thought I'd catch you at Harmony, see how you were doing." That was the truth, minus a few details.

"It's a good thing you followed me." Tears brimmed under her eyes, her voice thick. "Five more seconds and…"

She would have been dead. No way around it. They both knew it.

A fire truck swerved onto the shoulder, firefighters rushing toward her car with retardant, the sirens cutting off. Triss watched silently, emotionless. He couldn't figure her out. Every time she let him see a piece of her heart, she quickly hid behind a mask of indifference. It was that habit that had finally convinced him to let her keep the distance she was forever trying to expand between them. His kids had been confused and hurt when she'd disappeared from their lives months ago, and Hunter wouldn't put them through that disappointment again.

He was glad he'd come today, glad he'd been there at the right time. But it was time to get going. He figured he should call Luke in to take over.

A police officer approached the truck, and Hunter opened the door, stepping out. He immediately recognized the officer as a friend of Roman's they'd worked with in the past.

"Officer Goodson," Hunter said, offering a hand to the seasoned cop, noting his impeccable uniform and alert expression.

"Hunter." They shook hands, and Hunter motioned to Triss inside the cab.

"The Mustang is hers."

"Was," she muttered, leaning her head toward them to greet the officer.

"Doesn't look like you should have made it out of that alive," the officer commented. "Are you injured?"

"Not that I can tell."

"We've got paramedics on the scene. I'd encourage you to take a ride and get checked out at the hospital, anyway, after we speak."

"I'll see my doctor tomorrow if I need to," she said. "But I appreciate it."

"You should let them check you out at the hospital," Hunter suggested. "It was a pretty bad wreck."

She shook her head. "I'm fine."

"You could have internal—"

"Hunter."

She'd made her decision, and there was nothing he could say to change her mind. Her jaw was set, her lips pressed together. He knew the look when he saw it.

The officer ducked his head slightly so he could see her. "Tell me what happened."

Hunter listened with interest as she described hearing a distinct pop before she smelled smoke. He hadn't seen anything but the smoke, and he wondered what could have caused the pop. The interview was brief, and the officer handed her his card. Once again, he advised her to get checked out and to rest up, and then he returned to the scene.

"That was a sweet ride," Hunter said. "Looks like there's no saving it."

"No. But I'll have it towed to my mechanic, anyway. Hopefully, he can figure out what happened. I can't afford not to get anything from insurance."

The moments before the wreck played through Hunter's mind, the sudden smoke billowing at the rear of the car. "Wonder what could have caused that fire."

She was quiet for a moment too long, and then she shifted in her seat, pulling off his jacket and handing it to him before raising her seat straight. She was clearly ignoring his comment. "Would you mind driving me to Harmony after I get the car situation settled?"

"Hold on a minute," he said, searching her eyes for what he was missing.

She held his gaze, her expression unreadable. "What?"

"You're not telling me something."

She glanced away for a fraction of a second, and he knew he was right.

"What is it?" he persisted when she didn't respond.

She shook her head. "Probably nothing."

"Well, if that isn't the most overused and usually inaccurate phrase we hear in our line of work, I don't know what is."

It was a phrase used too often by victims of stalking and domestic violence, unsure whether they were in danger or out of their minds.

Triss sighed. "I know. But what I'm thinking sounds crazy." She stared into his eyes with conviction, as if willing him to believe what she was about to say.

He already did. He might still be rankled by how suddenly she'd dropped out of his life—out of his kids' lives—but that didn't change what he knew about her. She was intuitive, sharp and levelheaded. She was not prone to drama, exaggeration or misinterpretation. And if Triss Everett had something bizarre to say, she'd only say it if she knew it to be true.

"I can handle crazy."

Her eyes were dark, troubled in a way he'd never seen before. "I don't think what happened was an accident, Hunter," she said finally. "I think someone caused the fire. I think someone hoped I would die. And I think that same person may have killed before. At Harmony."

That, he hadn't expected. Hunter reached for what to ask next, and Triss narrowed her eyes.

"You said you could handle crazy." In a flash, she reached for the door. "I'm going to talk to the tow-truck driver."

"Hey." He slid his hand to her free arm, tugging her wrist gently to get her to stay. She looked at him, her eyes flashing annoyance. But, also, uncertainty. "I'm not going anywhere," he said, because it seemed like that was what she needed to hear, even if he thought it couldn't be more obvious. "But I'm going to need more details."

She yanked her wrist from his hand, but let go of the door handle, her attention flicking to the clock on the dashboard. "There's a lot to tell you. But I need to get to Harmony. There's the reception, and I need to—"

"The reception can go on without you, Triss. You've been in a major accident. I still think you should get checked out at the hospital."

She was already shaking her head and reaching for the door again. "I'm fine. Just let me talk to the tow-truck driver, and I'll give you more details on the drive back."

"Sure," he said more casually than he felt, pushing away a dark flash of memory from the night his wife had died. He should have called the ambulance sooner, or picked her up bodily and forced her to go to the hospital. His misjudgment had cost her her life. Now, he wished Triss would listen to him—but he was just a coworker and had no right to push her. Still, he wasn't without recourse. He couldn't force her to go to the hospital, but she couldn't force him to go home, either. And he wouldn't be heading home tonight until he was sure she was safe.

TWO

"Start at the beginning," Hunter said, pulling onto the interstate.

Twenty-five minutes of highway stretched between the cemetery and Harmony Senior Living. It wasn't enough time to explain all that had happened, but Triss never used more words than she had to, so she would make it work.

"The first person who died was Walter," Triss started. "Walter Tompkins. He was eighty-six. Diabetic coma while he slept. He never woke up. All the residents were talking about how it was the perfect way to go. Everyone wants to die in their sleep."

Hunter said nothing, so she continued. "Genevieve Hail was next. Her boyfriend always called her Jenna-Doll. She was sixty-seven. Heart attack during dialysis."

"Boyfriend?"

"Don. He's a resident, too. They'd been together about a year. He was planning to propose."

"How long after Walter?"

"Six days."

"Go on."

"Connie Mays, four days later. Walking pneumonia

got serious fast. She died while reading in her armchair. She was the healthiest seventy-two-year-old I'd ever met. And then, she was dead."

"And this time, Frank Townsend," Hunter said. "What was his story?"

"Ten days had passed. I'd started to think that the three deaths had been a tragic fluke. A bad season at Harmony. But Frank—he overdosed on prescription painkillers. He was one of the newer residents, always cheerful. Everyone loved him."

"People learn to hide their pain," Hunter pointed out.

"I won't argue with that. Another possibility is an accidental overdose. He was a bit of a drinker and he'd had a beer or two that day. His daughter also mentioned she thought he'd started to show signs of dementia. He was scheduled for an evaluation later this week."

Hunter nodded. "My mom suffered with dementia. Caught her consuming a whole stick of butter one day. She'd ingest anything that wasn't locked up."

"Exactly," Triss agreed. "Which is why I know this sounds crazy. There's a logical explanation for all of these deaths. But something doesn't sit right with me. That's a lot of death in a short amount of time."

"At a residential community for the elderly," Hunter added. He glanced over at her. "But?"

"But my gut tells me something else is going on," Triss responded.

She filled him in on the lax security at Harmony and her ideas for tightening it up—if for nothing else, then for her own peace of mind. She told him about the meeting she'd held two days ago to get the other grad students and some staff on board—and how no one seemed to take her concerns seriously. And she told him that she'd started to wonder if she simply was being paranoid and not dealing well with grief.

Hunter was mostly quiet as she told the story, but that was his way. She'd been with him on enough interviews to know how he operated. When drawing up security plans, he believed in long silences and letting clients tell their stories until they ran out of words. That's when he would start asking questions. She let silence fall over the car and waited.

Finally, Hunter glanced over at her. "This is a lot to handle alone," he said. "I would have backed you up at that meeting."

"We haven't exactly seen much of each other lately."

A beat passed, and she immediately regretted her words. It was no one's fault but her own that they hadn't seen much of each other. She had a phone. She had his number. She'd purposely stayed away.

"No," Hunter said. "We haven't."

She suspected he wanted to say more on that topic, but he didn't. Their exit was coming up, and he slowed, pulling off the highway. "So, four people have died in three weeks. On Monday, you held a security meeting and no one supported your ideas, and today your car catches on fire leaving the funeral."

"I told you it sounded crazy." She refused to look at him, afraid to see the doubt in his eyes. She could handle that look from almost anyone. But not from Hunter.

"It does sound crazy," he finally said, and her heart sank.

When did she get so soft? When had words gained

the power to hurt her again? Why did she care if Hunter believed her? It wasn't as if—

"But I believe you," Hunter added.

Relief flooded over Triss. The truck turned onto the winding road that led to the senior living community, fall leaves swirling along the path. She wanted to thank him. And hug him. Strangely, she also wanted to cry. She didn't do any of those things. Instead, as he pulled up to the security gate, she said, "Good. Now is when you help me figure out what to do next."

She gave him the code to open the wrought-iron gate, and as he drove through it and onto the property, he glanced her way. "The next order of business would be to file a report with the police. You may not have had much to go on with the residents' deaths, but what happened today definitely gives your concerns more credibility."

"Right."

"And upgrading security measures like you mentioned would be a reasonable next step."

The narrow road opened onto the well-manicured property, tufts of golden leaves scattered along the drive and the walkways.

"I'll get in touch with Roman tonight and see what we can pull together. They have a security team here?"

He pulled into a parking spot.

"Sort of. Two officers patrol on twelve-hour shifts. You can usually find one of them in the admin offices over there." She pointed to a small whitewashed brick cottage across the parking lot.

"Good. I'll try to get with one of them before I leave."

He turned off the truck and focused his attention on her. Triss forced herself to meet his gaze, to pretend that the warm concern in his soft brown eyes didn't affect her one bit.

"You sure you're okay? We can turn around now and get you checked out."

"I'm fine," she insisted, and she meant it. She hadn't hit her head, and she wasn't the least bit tired. She was overwhelmed. She'd almost died, and then Hunter had shown up—the man who had spent the past couple of years slowly chipping away at every wall Triss had built around her heart. The very man she'd been successfully avoiding since August.

She started to open the door, but Hunter reached past her and opened the glove box.

"Hold on." He pulled out a packet of wet wipes and handed them to her. "Unless you want to answer a bunch of questions, you'll want to get rid of the evidence." A hint of a smile played on his lips, and Triss flipped down the visor mirror.

Traces of smoke residue were smudged along the side of her nose and the edge of her jaw. She took a wipe and swiped it over her skin, erasing any signs of the accident. Then she grabbed a new one for her hands, a warm thankfulness rising at Hunter's thoughtfulness.

She handed the pack to him. "Better?"

His gaze traveled over her face, his eyes too soft. He nodded and popped the packet back in the compartment, which was also stuffed with a pack of crackers, two Pull-Ups and a box of Disney-character Band-Aids.

He glanced up at her as he closed the console, humor in his expression as he caught her observing.

"It's my emergency stash," he said.

Somehow, the stash made her heart ache, but Triss forced a small smile. "Always prepared."

Of course, he would be as a single dad of two young kids.

She opened the door and stepped out, pushing away the emotions threatening to rise again. What was wrong with her?

Death. Funerals. Families weeping over graves.

And Hunter, crouching on the hood of her car, locking eyes with her and renewing her strength as her breath started to fail, just as her body started to give up.

If she was the type of woman who dreamed of happily-ever-afters, he was the type of man she would dream about. Courageous, quick and smart at work. Tender and lighthearted with his kids. Kind to everyone he met.

Of course, Triss wasn't prone to dreaming. Even if she was, Hunter was off-limits, and she would never tell him why. The reminder wrenched at her heart as Hunter came around the front of the truck and walked alongside her. Sure, she'd moved here to cut her expenses and get out of her brother's house. But the move had also allowed her to cut her hours at Shield and switch to the weekend night shift, which meant she rarely saw Hunter. And that had been on purpose.

"My mom lived here when her dementia got bad."

Triss glanced over at Hunter as they headed up the walkway toward Creekside Manor, the independent-living home where Triss resided. Harmony was set on fifty wooded acres with walking trails, gardens, a man-made lake and a fitness center, and offered fresh, or-ganic meals and live music twice a week. There were three separate homes for residents. Creekside was for those who could still live independently, and the resi-dents resided in either single- or double-bed apartments. Silverwood Villa housed assisted-living and memory-care residents. Emerald Estate was the last stop, so to speak, with skilled nursing care available 24/7.

"This is the place to be when you can't live on your own anymore," Triss commented.

Hunter agreed. "Mom seemed to enjoy it. She started in Silverwood until she moved into Emerald."

His voice had lowered, his gaze roaming over the property as they walked. "How many of the deaths were at Creekside?" he asked.

"All of them."

He raised his eyebrows.

"Exactly." The deaths might not have been as wor-risome or noticeable if they'd happened between the three homes, or mostly in Silverwood and Emerald, but all the residents had died at Creekside—where no one required nursing care. In fact, there had only been one other death since Triss had moved in, and it was over at Emerald in September.

A car parked nearby, a young family climbing out, likely coming to visit parents and grandparents, and Triss figured she and Hunter probably shouldn't dis-cuss murder suspicions out in the open.

"How long did your mom live here?" she asked, moving into more neutral territory.

"Four years. She passed away when Josie was two."

"Young for dementia, right?"

He nodded. "Sixty-three at onset. She was never the same after my dad died. He was twelve years older, a smoker. Died of lung cancer."

Triss knew loss. She also knew that Hunter had been an only child, and she could read the latent grief in his eyes. She was scrambling to think of something to say other than "I'm sorry," but the doors flew open in front of them and Kaye Lawson emerged, her bright red lipstick matching her wide smile and fiery hair. Kaye had moved into Harmony after a stroke, determined not to burden any of her six children, and despite her nearly full recovery, she'd stayed.

"There you are!" Kaye was a thin woman, but tall, and she wrapped Triss in a motherly hug. Triss had finally stopped avoiding Kaye's hugs several weeks ago. She couldn't remember what it felt like to be hugged by her own mother, an addict who had been in and out of jail for decades, bringing home questionable men and leaving for days at a time. Kaye claimed that Triss needed more hugs, and Triss was starting to think she may be right.

"Sorry I'm late," Triss offered, not mentioning the accident. She didn't want to draw the attention away from the celebration of Frank's life and onto her.

"We were starting to worry about you." The woman's observant gaze seemed to inspect Triss with a question, but she didn't ask it. Instead, she glanced curiously toward Hunter. "Now, who is this handsome young man?"

Hunter flashed his disarmingly charming and dimpled smile at Kaye. "Hunter Knox." He held out a hand, but Kaye laughed.

"I only accept hugs."

Hunter laughed, too, hugging her in greeting and sending a good-natured wink at Triss. She felt a smile tugging, her pulse suddenly racing. She looked away. This was exactly why she was trying to get some distance from him. All her defenses were useless when he was nearby.

"Hunter and I work together at Shield," Triss said as they all walked inside. "Hunter, this is my friend Kaye."

"Are you helping set up?" Kaye asked him.

"He doesn't have much time," Triss answered for him, helping him off the hook. "You have to get home for the kids, right?"

"I have time."

"I like you already." Kaye smiled broadly, her face a map of lines that showed she lived a life bent toward joy and maybe adventure.

"So, you have kids," Kaye said, leading the way through the common area. "How old are they?"

"My daughter, Josie, is about to turn six. And my son, Levi, is two."

"Oh, and I'm sure they keep you on your toes. If your wife's at home holding down the fort, you'd better not stay here too long," she said with a grin.

Kaye's gaze flicked to Triss, and Triss groaned inwardly. Knowing Kaye, she'd already searched for

Hunter's wedding band, found it missing and decided she'd found Triss a husband.

"Their very young and energetic nanny is home with them, and she's paid very well," he said warmly. "My wife passed away after our son was born."

Kaye's smile fell. "Oh, dear. How sad." She touched his arm. "I'm sure you're a wonderful dad."

"Thank you." He smiled ruefully. "Some days I do better than others."

"That's parenthood for you. You should bring them by some time. We love kids around here. So much energy."

"I've been meaning to for a while now, actually," he said. "We'd visit sometimes when my mother was here a few years ago."

"Well, Brandon's over there setting up the microphone." She pointed to the front of the room near the fireplace, where a white-haired gentleman was crouched in front of a microphone stand, his back to the room. "He's our activities director. You should talk to him."

"Sounds good. I'll catch up with you two in...?"

"The kitchen or dining hall," Triss suggested, and then followed Kaye.

"Let's get the waters filled on the tables," Kaye said. "Then we'll light the centerpiece candles."

"Got it."

The dining hall was quiet, and a handful of residents were starting to trickle in. Triss glanced around as she filled water glasses, her focus returning now that Hunter was out of the picture. What had happened with her car had heightened her suspicions. She shifted her gaze to each new guest that entered—residents, care-givers, custodial staff, her fellow grad students. No one seemed to be paying her much attention. If anyone knew she'd been in a life-threatening accident, they weren't letting on.

Her pitcher ran out again and she headed to the kitchen, standing at the fridge to fill it with filtered water.

"How's it going out there?"

Triss glanced over at Barb, Creekside's live-in chef, noting that she'd exchanged her trademark blue apron with smiling cartoon bananas for a plain black one more appropriate for the occasion.

"Good. People are starting to arrive. Need any help in here?"

Barb shook her head. "I've got it under control. The family wanted chicken alfredo, though—sorry, there's not much of a substitute for that."

"I'll stick with the salad," Triss said. "You know I've told you not to worry about me." She had a pretty serious dairy allergy that had necessitated an EpiPen more than once in her life, and Barb couldn't stand the idea of anyone missing out on a meal.

"I made a couple of chicken-and-rice meals for you. They're in the fridge if you get hungry later."

For a split second, Triss wanted to set down the pitcher and hug Barb. But that would be awkward for both of them, so she just said, "Thank you," knowing that Barb couldn't possibly understand how touching her thoughtfulness was. More days than she could count, there had been no food in the Everett household when she was younger. Luke was forever scavenging leftovers from restaurants and grocery stores for the three siblings to split, and a well-meaning neighbor sometimes dropped groceries by. It was a wonder Triss had survived those years. She learned many years later that Luke had scoured ingredients labels on the grocery leftovers and had made friends with two local restaurant owners, who saved dairy-free extras regularly for them. They'd had one scare, when she was six, but Luke had managed to get her to a hospital. They'd left with two separate foster families, Triss with an EpiPen. It was the first time they'd been split up—Cal and Luke to one home, and Triss to another. They'd been more careful after that.

With the pitcher topped off, Triss turned from the kitchen, pushing the swinging door open with her arm as Hunter walked in.

She stopped short, water sloshing from the pitcher onto his white button-down.

"Whoa." He grasped the pitcher, steadying it as Triss took a quick step backward.

"Sorry," she said, water dripping along her arms, a bubble of laughter threatening at the amused expression on Hunter's face.

He took the pitcher from her. "Here." Reaching past her, he grabbed a hand towel and wiped the sides of the pitcher before handing it to her. The tips of his fingers grazed her hand, sending a sudden jolt of awareness straight up her arms.

So. It hadn't been shock earlier, when he'd lifted her into his arms and every muscle in her body had gone weak, her pulse racing as her hand had clutched a small square of his shirt. It had simply been the effect Hunter had on her. What was it about him?

"You talked to Brandon?" she asked, realizing she'd stood still for a couple of seconds too long.

He nodded. "He said I can bring the kids any day between lunch and dinner—just shoot him an email."

"Great. Heading home?"

"Figured I'd help out." He took off his wet tie and shoved it in a pocket, then started unbuttoning his shirt cuffs and rolling up his sleeves.

"I think we've got things under control," Triss said, making a move toward the door. "You need to—"

"I'm planning to stick around for a while. I can sit and observe, but I'd much rather have something to do," Hunter said, moving in front of her and blocking her path as he rolled up the second sleeve.

"Give the man a job, Triss, and out you both go! Too many cooks in my kitchen."

Triss shot a glare over at Barb even as the woman winked at Hunter and continued prepping several large salads.

"We're setting tables," Triss said finally. She pointed to an empty pitcher by the sink. "Go ahead and fill that one up with ice water and meet me in the dining hall." She scooted past him and turned out of the kitchen.

Hunter hurried to the pitcher, filling it and heading out the way he'd seen Triss turn. He wanted to tell her to slow down, to sit, to take it easy. But he knew any suggestions wouldn't just be ignored, they'd be fought.

The best he could do would be to stay close, keep an eye on her. Was he overreacting? Maybe. But he'd learned two years ago exactly what could happen when physical symptoms were ignored. His wife had died because of it.

When he turned into the dining hall, he noticed Triss setting down her pitcher and taking a seat next to one of the residents. She leaned forward, empathy in her expression as she listened.

Hunter filled the glasses around the room, his attention flicking to Triss as he did so. She spoke softly to the man, whose dark hair was still winning its battle against gray. Her hand came to the man's upper arm, soothingly rubbing it as the man wiped away tears. Her tenderness was always a surprise when she let it show, and Hunter wondered often why she worked so hard to hide it.

He'd been intrigued by Triss ever since he'd met her at the gun range during a training session a couple of years ago. She'd never shot a gun in her life, but within hours she was outshooting police veterans. He'd been impressed, but not drawn to her in the least. The loss of his wife was still raw, and Triss emanated no warmth. She didn't smile even once, and barely spoke the entire day, moving off to the side to eat a quick bagged lunch she'd brought, clearly signaling she wasn't interested in conversation.

She was gorgeous, with a slim athletic figure, and wide dark eyes set against caramel skin. But her body language created a barrier that told people she was intensely private and happier that way. Still, something about her intrigued Hunter, especially when he learned that Luke was her older brother. Luke had to be one of the most congenial guys Hunter had ever met, and the contrast between the two was striking—even though their sibling bond was obvious to anyone who saw them together.

Over time, their friendship grew, and Hunter had become determined to discover what had hurt her so much in the past that she had created a rigid wall around her. She had seemed just as determined to keep her distance, which had become painfully obvious when she'd moved to Harmony and stopped contacting Hunter in August. Even his kids had started getting attached to her, and her disappearance had been confusing for them.

But something had shifted between them today. His mind called up the memory of her in his arms, her hand clutching his shirt. He'd never known Triss to accept help, but she had done more than accept his help. She had hung on to him, her face pressed to his chest.

And he hadn't missed her reaction when he'd run into her in the kitchen doorway a few minutes ago. Triss, flustered? Was it possible he still had a chance to deepen the friendship he'd been fighting for? Did he even want to? The last thing he wanted to do was disappoint his kids if she started coming around and then disappeared again. And Triss had big goals, he reminded himself.

When she'd signed the contract at Harmony and essentially made an exit from his life, he'd told himself that he wouldn't get in the way of her dreams, like he had with his late wife. Viv never did finish college and go on to practice law like she'd planned to do. If he was honest with himself, he was the one who had pushed for the marriage. She would have been content to finish out her education first and have kids later. But she'd caved to his cajoling, lost in the glamour of the romance and the lure of a future together...before her entire life was stolen from her a few short years later. He wouldn't do that to someone else, especially not to Triss.

It wasn't something he should be thinking about, anyway. Not after what Triss had told him today. He'd stick around for a while and observe what was going on, then have a chat with Security before heading home to the kids. Thankfully, he had flexible childcare.

Hiring a live-in nanny had been the best decision he'd made since his wife's death. A college student and the oldest of five kids, Samantha Farrow knew her way around the kitchen, the laundry room, temper tantrums and messy diapers. What was more—she genuinely seemed to adore his kids. Granted, Josie and Levi were pretty easy to get along with. But he'd had sitters before who had been all too eager to plop the kids in front of a television or cart them off to bed early. Samantha enjoyed interacting with them, playing games with them, reading to them, teaching them—which meant that Hunter could focus his energy on keeping an eye on Triss tonight, knowing his kids were in good hands.

The next half hour slipped by quickly, as the tables were set, the buffet was spread out and the guests arrived. Triss gave Hunter new tasks when he asked, but for the most part, she didn't seem to notice that he was there. All her energy and emotion seemed focused on making the reception run smoothly, as she spoke with residents and also Frank's family members. Despite her typically guarded nature, she knew how to draw someone into a conversation, her sincerity evident in her body language and the softness that had fallen over her expression. She might be living here on a contract, but she wasn't merely fulfilling her duty or putting on a show to prove that she was worthy of the position. She genuinely cared, and for some reason, Hunter's heart swelled as he watched her in action.

This was the part of her personality he'd caught glimpses of over the past couple of years, but something changed when she walked through the doors of Creekside, and her shields came down. Interesting.

By the time dinner was served, Hunter felt confident that Triss wasn't seriously injured or in any immediate danger. Plus, Triss knew how to handle herself. He glanced at his watch. Just enough time to touch base with Security and pick up groceries before heading home to tuck in his kids. He turned to leave the dining hall, but Kaye saw him and practically jumped out of her seat.

"You've helped all this time. Why don't you eat with us?" she suggested, grabbing his arm and attempting to pull him toward the buffet tables.

"I've got to get home, but thank you."

"Oh, right. Your kids are waiting for you. Well, I hope I'll get to meet them. Did you talk to Brandon?"

"I did. I'll bring the kids by soon."

"Levi and Josie, right? I can't wait."

"Have a good night, Kaye," he said and started to turn

away before he had a last-minute thought. "Actually…"
He pulled out his wallet, slipped out a business card and
handed it to her. "I'm a little worried about Triss. I don't
think she wants anyone to know right now, but I'd feel
better if someone here was watching out for her. She was
in an accident on the way back from the cemetery today."

Kaye accepted the card, her eyes widening. "That's
why she seemed different when she walked in. Why
she was late…"

"She didn't want to go to the hospital, so I was keeping an eye on her. Would you—"

Kaye was already nodding. "I have six daughters.
This is my specialty." She smiled then, tapping the card.
"What a very caring *coworker* you are."

Hunter couldn't help but grin. The woman was as-
tute, and he knew he could trust her to watch out for
Triss.

"Go home to your kiddos, now. And I won't tell Triss
that I know about the accident." She gave him a goodbye hug and Hunter let himself out of the home, heading across the parking lot to the cottage-like building
Triss had pointed out.

The cottage was constructed of whitewashed brick,
and its oak door was unlocked. Hunter tapped on it before opening the door, and was greeted by a jungle of
flowers and a smiling silver-haired woman snipping
thorns off of a pile of roses. The place smelled like a
flower boutique, with arrangements in a myriad of vases
on every surface.

"Hello there," the woman said, her voice chipper.
"How can I help you?"

"Sorry," Hunter said, confused. The place looked more like a gift shop than an administrative office building. "I think I'm in the wrong place. I was looking for Security."

"Oh, no. You're in the right place. I'm the office manager." The woman set aside her flowers and wiped her hands on a hand towel before offering a handshake to Hunter. "Laura Senate. My daughter's wedding is this weekend, and I'm helping make the floral arrangements."

"You do beautiful work."

"Thank you. The security office is around the corner. First door on the left." She pointed, but a frown line surfaced along her forehead. "I hope everything's okay?"

"I have a few questions I wanted to run by the team."

The woman nodded, still not quite smiling. "Vince's there right now, and Adam's somewhere…" She shrugged. "It's pretty quiet out here, you know."

"It's a peaceful place," Hunter agreed. "Thanks for the help." He followed her instructions and walked around the corner, finding the first door on the left open. He tapped on the wall outside the door and peeked in.

The man at the desk wore black slacks and a gray uniform shirt A brown desk plaque gave the name *Vince Beck*. He looked up from his computer monitor in surprise, his hand coming up to adjust his too-long combover.

"Yes?" the man asked, his gruff voice matching his bulky frame.

Hunter stepped into the room and held out a hand,

"I'm Hunter Knox. A friend of mine is one of the graduate students here at Harmony—Triss Everett."

Vince smiled and relaxed, shaking Hunter's hand. "How can I help you?"

Without much information yet, Hunter wanted to be careful with his words. His purpose tonight was to get a feel for the security at Harmony, and also the receptiveness of the team to making some adjustments.

"You may know that Triss works for Shield Protection Services. We're coworkers, actually."

Vince's expression was suddenly amused. "Oh, yes, we all know about Triss and her focus on security. She's always got new ideas she wants us to put in place, but Harmony hasn't ever had a security problem. I say, if it ain't broke, why fix it?"

Hunter didn't see the humor Vince obviously saw, and took note that he would likely meet resistance when trying to implement any changes. Vince seemed a little too comfortable with his job. He was a big guy, probably in his late thirties. He carried a little extra weight around his midsection, but otherwise he appeared fit. He didn't wear a wedding ring, and there were no family photos anywhere in his office.

Hunter forced a smile. "It's a beautiful place. My mom was here for a while." He started. "Maybe you knew her—Wendy Knox?"

Vince shook his head. "Doesn't ring a bell, but I've only been here three years."

Hunter nodded. "She passed before that, but sure enjoyed her time here. In fact, I know others who are considering it for their parents. Would you mind giving me a quick rundown of your security protocols?"

"Oh, sure," Vince said, motioning for Hunter to take a seat as he turned a wide-screen computer monitor toward him. The monitor showed four grainy scenes at a time. "This here's our monitor," Vince began, and Hunter suppressed a sigh. This was going to be worse than he'd expected.

A half hour later, Hunter was thinking about the practically nonexistent security at Harmony and wondering how quickly Shield could convince Harmony management to make improvements. A private security company, Shield designed, installed and manned custom security systems for residences and businesses. Due to the nature of the work, agents often served as both bodyguards and investigators, reporting suspicious activity and passing tips on to police. Usually, potential clients approached Shield for help. Bringing a proposal to Harmony would likely be a hard sell. Maybe bringing his kids to the facility the next day would be a good first step. That way, he could get a feel for the place without making anyone uneasy.

He pulled into the first grocery store he saw, heading quickly inside and grabbing a basket. He'd only managed to grab bananas and frozen chicken nuggets when his cell phone rang, the number unfamiliar.

"Hello?" he answered, snagging a pack of mini doughnuts for his kids in the morning.

"Is this Hunter Knox?" a woman's voice asked.

He recognized the voice, and his heart pitched. "Yes.

What's wrong, Kaye?" He was setting his basket on a closed register before she could even answer, heading straight for the exit.

"It's Triss. She just left the dining hall. I followed her and she told me she was very tired. Unlike her. It's not even seven o'clock. And she looked…funny."

"Funny, how?"

"I can't really say. Her eyes looked kind of glazed. Maybe I'm overreacting…"

"I'm heading back now."

"Hurry, okay?"

"You got it." Hunter was already running to his truck. He slammed the door shut and peeled out of the parking lot.

This is what he'd been afraid of—a head injury or an internal injury that hadn't made itself known immediately. He should have forced her to get checked out after the accident. Well, she wouldn't argue with him this time. He would go over there and knock on her door until she opened it, and then he was going to drive her straight to the hospital—even if he had to drag her.

THREE

Kaye was waiting for Hunter on the porch, a young man at her side.

"She won't answer her phone or her door," Kaye told him as she turned back to Creekside Manor. "We called 911."

The man next to her opened the door for them.

"Do we have a key to her room?" Hunter asked.

"Stella—she's the owner—said we can't open it until the police arrive," Kaye said. "She thinks I'm overreacting."

"She's only been in her room fifteen minutes," the young man pointed out, and Hunter glanced over at him as they headed down the hall together. He wore black Adidas pants and a white compression shirt, as if he was heading out or coming from the gym. His hair was dark, thick and gelled up high with the ends bleached blond.

"I'm Zach," the guy volunteered. "I'm one of the student residents."

"Did you see Triss?" Hunter asked.

Zach shook his head. "I mean, I saw her today, but she seemed fine. I was just keeping Kaye company."

"He didn't think I should call 911, either," Kaye said, her thin lips pressing together, the lipstick from earlier long since faded. She was worried, like a mother would be, her hands clasped tightly in front of her as they hurried to Triss's room.

"When did you call?"

"Just before you pulled in. I couldn't wait any longer. Something's wrong, I know it."

When they reached Triss's apartment, Hunter rang the bell, and then pounded on the door loud enough to wake anyone on the entire property who might be taking a nap.

"What's going on?" a voice called from the commons, and footsteps hurried down the hall.

"That's Stella," Kaye said.

"Good."

Hunter met the woman and extended a hand in greeting. "I'm Hunter Knox, Triss's friend. We need to get into her apartment."

Stella stared calmly up at him. She was more than a foot shorter than Hunter, but wasn't at all intimidated. She shook his hand. "Hunter, I'm Stella. I appreciate that you're a friend of Triss's, but I don't know you from Harry. As I told Kaye, we'll need to wait for the police to get here. For all we know, Triss left the building and no one saw her. Maybe that's why she's not answering."

"No. I've been watching her door." Kaye lifted her chin in argument. "And calling her."

"Well, I know for a fact you left the door a couple of times, because—"

"Look," Hunter interrupted. "I don't want to waste

any more time. We have two options here. You can either give me the key to her room and let me take the
fall for breaking and entering if she decides to bring
charges, or I can break this door down and pay for the
damages later. One way or another, I'm getting in this
room, and I'm not waiting for the police."

Stella's eyes narrowed, anger and alarm in her expression. "I think I'm going to have to go with option
number three," she said, taking a step back. "I'll need
to call Security."

She turned on her heel and started to walk away.
That was fine with Hunter. He'd get the door open before Security arrived, and then, if Triss needed help,
she'd get it.

He tested the door, sliding a credit card up the jamb
and noting that she'd locked the dead bolt. He'd have
to break it down.

"Just give him the key, Stella!" someone shouted.
"Poor Triss wouldn't want her door smashed!"

Hunter looked over and realized that several residents had gathered in the hall, as well as a handful of
staff, all watching with a mixture of surprise and horror.

Stella hesitated, and so did Hunter.

"Yeah, give him the key," a gentleman said, and
Hunter recognized him as the emotional man Triss had
been speaking with earlier at the reception. "We need
to make sure she's okay."

"Policy is that—"

"Do you smell that?" Kaye interrupted just as the
odor registered with Hunter.

Smoke.

"Oh, no!" Kaye exclaimed, pointing to the bottom of the door, where a barely visible stream of smoke curled upward into the hallway.

"Hcrc!" Stclla moved forward and thrust the key into Hunter's hand.

Wasting no time, he unlocked the door and opened it into smoke so thick and hot that he reared back, coughing.

"Get everyone out!" he yelled behind him, but the crowd was already scrambling for the exits. He shrugged off his jacket, then pressed it to his mouth and nose as a makeshift mask as he entered the hazy apartment. Why wasn't the smoke alarm going off? Where was Triss?

Fire licked up the wall of the kitchen, spreading fast. Hunter ignored the sting of smoke in his eyes and all the common sense that told him to get out now and hope the fire department arrived in time. That wasn't an option. Not until he knew Triss wasn't there.

The small living room was empty and he raced to the adjoining door, which he assumed led to her bedroom.

He swung the door open, almost expecting it to be empty. Hoping, at this point, that it would be. That Triss was long gone and far away from the fire. But in the dark, as smoke billowed into the room, a shadow of a figure was visible on the bed.

He rushed in. Triss was lying on top of the covers, on her side, her funeral clothes and boots still on.

"Triss!" He quickly turned her onto her back, knew he didn't have much time. Her arm fell to her side— her body was slack but warm to the touch. A good sign.

Probably a concussion, he told himself, though doubt lingered. She hadn't shown any signs of a concussion, and hadn't said she'd hit her head.

No time to dwell on questions. He scooped her into his arms and ran out to the living room as fire crackled and shot across the doorway. He maneuvered around the fire, losing his battle for breath. The door to the hallway beckoned, even as his steps slowed. He couldn't gather a breath, and he nearly fell just yards from the hallway.

But the faces of his children flashed through his mind and he silently begged for strength from the God he rarely talked to. He was moments from losing all ability to escape…and then he was in the hall, the smoke still thick but clearing.

Sirens sounded loudly outside the facility, and Hunter ran for an exit, cradling Triss close to his chest until he stumbled outside, cold air hitting him with stark relief. A cough took hold, and he moved across the lawn farther from the facility until he'd found the edge of the parking lot, where a crowd of residents and staff had gathered.

"Is she okay?" Kaye asked, rushing up to him as he lowered himself to the curb, keeping a secure hold on Triss.

A fire engine pulled into the lot, followed by an ambulance and police cruiser.

"I don't know," Hunter said as his coughs subsided and he looked at Triss's face. "But she's breathing."

He set a hand to Triss's forehead, then to the top of her scalp, feeling for any lump he couldn't see. Nothing out of the ordinary, he thought, as her silky hair tangled in his fingers. She seemed to be in a deep sleep, though. He was hoping it was a concussion, because other internal injuries could mean worse. But at least she'd escaped the fire. A shudder ran along his spine and he gently pushed her hair away from her eyes. If Kaye hadn't called... He shook his head, refusing to consider what could have happened. Paramedics were heading toward them with a stretcher, and as he helped maneuver her onto the gurney, he told himself that she was going to be okay. Only a little while ago, she'd been perfectly fine, eating and chatting and helping at the reception. She was in good hands, and he'd done everything he could do.

But experience told him that sometimes doing everything in his power wasn't good enough, and as he took a seat in the ambulance next to her, dread tightened in the pit of his stomach. If he'd learned nothing else from his wife's death, he'd learned that bad things happened that sometimes no one could control. He clenched his fists, staring at Triss's closed eyes, her slack jaw, her wild hair, and he hoped—even conceded to pray—that she would pull through.

Triss had woken up in hospitals enough to recognize where she was. The question was—why?

A hand squeezed hers, and she looked to her right, her brother's face coming into focus.

"Hey," Luke said quietly. "You're awake."

He leaned over her, his dark brown eyes searching her face for answers.

"What happened?" she asked, her voice raw.

"We're not sure. Your friend Kaye called Hunter and told him that you'd gotten suddenly tired and your eyes looked strange. He found you unconscious on your bed."

Triss frowned, reaching for memories of the afternoon. "Hunter?"

"Remember the car accident?"

The accident. Scenes flashed in her mind. The car bursting into flames. Hunter carrying her to his truck, then following her around at Harmony, pretending he wanted to help. But he'd been watching her, worried.

"I do. And I remember the reception." She searched for images, memories. "But I don't remember going to my room."

"We're still waiting on some labs. So far, the MRI and CT scans came up clear. They were worried about internal injuries from the wreck." He reached over and pressed the call button on her hospital bed.

"How can I help you?" a voice asked through the speaker.

"Triss woke up. The nurse asked me to notify her."

"She'll be right down."

"I'd better text Hunter. I made him go home two hours ago."

Triss's heart jumped. "He was here?"

"Rode in the ambulance with you. Stayed until I got here and wouldn't go home." Luke glanced up from his phone. There was a question in his eyes, but he didn't ask it, and Triss wasn't going to volunteer anything.

There was nothing to volunteer.

She liked Hunter.

A lot.

He reminded her of everything she'd always craved in a relationship but didn't believe she deserved. He'd married the love of his life fresh out of high school, and when she'd passed away shortly after the birth of their second child, he hadn't missed a beat in becoming the kind of dad who is always present and loving. He was a hard worker, a man of integrity, and his patience and sense of humor when it came to his kids was something that Triss had not witnessed often. Spending time with him and his little family always made her heart ache over what she could have had if she'd been brave enough to tell Luke the truth.

"You know, you'll give me a heart attack if you keep winding up in the hospital," Luke said.

Triss smirked, despite herself. She'd had quite a run of hospital emergencies since becoming a Shield agent. "You're the most levelheaded guy I've ever known. A few ER visits can't touch that."

His phone dinged and he glanced at it. "Hunter's on his way."

Triss squinted at the clock, unable to make out the time in the dark room. "What time is it?"

"Twelve thirty."

"In the morning?"

Luke nodded. "You were out for hours."

She stared up at him. There was something about his body language. Something he wasn't telling her. He was tapping a finger on his leg, his gaze moving around the room. Luke had practically raised her and their brother, Cal, minus the years they'd spent bouncing around in foster care. He'd become their legal guardian when he was twenty-one and she was ten. He was easy to read. She was about to ask him what was up when the door opened and a petite nurse walked in, her smile kind. She wore her hair in a large, gorgeous bun of thick, black braids.

"Hello, Ms. Triss," she said with a lilting foreign accent as she came to her bedside. Triss couldn't place the accent, but there was something nurturing and genuine in the tone and inflection. "My name is Bethlehem, but you can call me Betty." She set a gentle hand on Triss's shoulder. "How are we feeling? You took a nice, long nap, yes?"

Triss relaxed, immediately at ease. "I feel okay. A little light-headed."

"Any pain anywhere?"

"Just a headache, but it's mild."

Betty nodded. "Good, good. I have notified the doctor you are awake. He is on his way up. Would you like some water?"

"Please." She was unusually thirsty. And nervous, to be honest. What had landed her in the hospital? If the scans were all clear, what else could have caused her to lose consciousness? And why couldn't she remember anything after consoling George Wyrick before the reception began?

Betty poured a cup of water and handed it to her. "You ring me if you need me," she said. "I'm glad to see you awake and talking. And I'm sure your brother is, too." She patted Luke's back. "You have a good brother here, yes, you do."

Triss suppressed an eye roll at Luke's amused smile. "He doesn't let me forget it."

Betty grinned and started for the door, but stopped. "Where's that handsome young man-friend that came with her?"

"On his way," Luke said, and Betty nodded with satisfaction.

"He's a good man, too, he is."

She left the room, pulling the door closed behind her.

Triss looked at Luke, setting her attention on him. "What aren't you telling me?"

His finger stopped tapping, a beat passing as his eyes focused on the bag of fluid attached to her IV. She was right. He was keeping something from her.

"You may as well tell me now. I'm not some delicate flower, Luke."

Luke laughed at that, his attention shifting back to her. "Never accused you of being one." But then his smile fell, and his gaze turned serious. "There was a fire. In your apartment."

She pushed herself up, her pulse racing. "What? How?"

"Looks like you left your stovetop on—a rag was too close."

She was shaking her head as he told her, denial rising alongside horror.

"Was everyone…?"

"Everyone got out. Hunter got you out just in time. Firefighters contained the fire to your apartment."

Hunter ran in to save her? Her eyes stung unexpectedly. Of course he had. Hunter was the kind of man who risked all for others…but he had kids to take care of. Her thoughts shifted back to the previous day, but she knew she hadn't turned on that stove. She lived by a routine she rarely changed. Each morning before school she ate a quick breakfast with the early risers in the dining hall, jogged the two miles to campus, ran the bleachers ten times, spent thirty minutes at the campus gym and went to class. She took the bus back for lunch, and usually ate dinner with the residents as well. She almost never cooked.

She definitely hadn't cooked yesterday. And she would never leave the stove on with a rag nearby.

Her mind raced. The car accident. The unconsciousness. The fire. The four dead residents.

"There's no way I—"

A soft knock tapped at the door and a man in a white lab coat walked in, a stethoscope around his neck. He smiled pleasantly and held a hand out to Triss.

"I'm Dr. O'Neill. How are you feeling, Triss?"

He glanced at her monitors, stepping in closer to her, probably noting that her heart was about to leap right out of her chest.

"I feel fine, really. Just a headache."

But she didn't feel fine at all. Her mind whirled with questions. Something was wrong at Harmony, and she was sure of it. But who would believe her? Who would target the residents of the senior living community? And why turn on Triss?

By the time the doctor had left, she only felt worse. They'd run all the standard tests, and nothing had shown up in her scans or the labs to explain the spell of unconsciousness. She'd be discharged with instructions to follow up with her family doctor.

She turned to Luke, bursting with all the suspicions filtering through her mind, but Hunter walked in, and her breath caught in her throat. Why was it that her heart skipped a beat every time he showed up? She'd told her heart to keep him out, but it seemed an impossible feat.

He approached her bedside, tired, unusually serious, his hand just touching her shoulder before he seemed to catch himself, and he shoved his hands in his jeans pockets. "How are you doing?"

She looked from Hunter to Luke, two men she knew she could trust with her life. Ignoring his question, she blurted out what had been nagging at her mind for long minutes now. "I didn't use the stove yesterday. I was hardly in the kitchen all week."

"We were afraid of that," Hunter said. "I'll put in a call to Officer Goodson." He glanced at Luke. "Did you get a hold of Roman?"

Triss's attention jerked to her brother as she realized that Hunter had filled him in on what had been going on.

Luke nodded. "He'll be by in another hour or two. We'll get a plan in place before Triss is discharged."

Triss listened as the two exchanged ideas about how to best ensure her safety, and part of her wanted to chime in and remind them that she was part of the team, too. That she was in the room and had plenty of ideas to offer. But a warmth had settled over her, an unfamiliar sense of security that rose from the knowledge that she was taken care of. It had been a long time since she'd let anyone take care of her, and her eyelids felt so heavy. She'd let them work out the details tonight. Her eyes drifted closed, her heart settling into the slow rhythm of sleep, reassured by the cadence of their murmuring voices. Tomorrow, she'd be on her feet and ready to take back some control.

FOUR

The sun hadn't yet risen when Hunter arrived at the hospital. Just ahead, a Shield SUV pulled into a parking spot, and Roman stepped out. Hunter quickly parked and hopped out of his truck, catching up as Roman approached the hospital entrance. Their breath swirled in the frigid morning air.

"Luke said he'd meet us in the waiting room," Roman said in greeting. "Bryan got here a little early to keep an eye on her room."

The doors slid open in front of them, the heat from the building immediately cutting through the chill. "Good work yesterday," Roman said as they strode along the quiet hallway.

"Right time, right place," Hunter said, knowing full well that he'd only done what any other Shield agent would have done.

"Good thing you went to the funeral."

"Thought Triss might want some support."

Roman glanced his way, open curiosity in his dark eyes. The guy didn't miss much and had probably detected whatever it was that had been sizzling between Hunter and Triss for the last year or so. "Luke and I had discussed going but thought she might be more annoyed than grateful."

Hunter couldn't help but grin at that. "You're probably right. Technically, I didn't even make it to the funeral. I got to the cemetery as Triss was leaving."

"And then she couldn't be annoyed because you swooped in and saved her life," Roman added, amusement lighting his eyes.

The waiting room was just ahead, and Luke was heading toward them as they turned into it. They were the only three people in the small room, a private waiting area usually reserved for family, and Luke closed the door before taking a seat in one of the burgundy vinyl chairs across from Hunter and Roman.

"How's she doing?" Hunter asked.

"Still asleep. She'll be discharged by noon. Waiting for more test results."

"Any leads?" Roman asked.

Luke shook his head. "No. But I got Goodson down here earlier. He's on it. He's getting the car processed, and he's got people combing through her apartment. The doctors are running toxicology tests to rule out the possibility she was drugged. That's what we're waiting on now. With clear scans and no signs of concussion, they seem to be at a loss."

Hunter mentally reviewed the previous evening. With so many people milling around and Triss bustling around the room, there would have been ample opportunity for someone to slip a drug into her drink, he supposed, but it didn't seem likely.

"Good," Roman said with a satisfied nod. "Now, let's talk strategy." He turned to Hunter. "Luke filled me in on Triss's suspicions, and I know you spent a little time at Harmony yesterday. What did you find out about their security?"

"Nonexistent," Hunter said. "There's a gate, but anyone can walk in or climb over the fencing, and two neighborhoods adjoin the property. To enter with a vehicle, people need a code, or they need to ask Security to let them in, and they register at the administration office."

"So anyone with a code has unrestricted access?" Roman asked.

"Right."

"What about cameras?" Luke asked.

"Security cameras in a handful of locations, but mostly outdoors, and they're not monitored constantly. Four security officers paired on rotating twelve-hour shifts on a fifty-acre property with at least sixty people on-site on any given day, sometimes many more."

Roman let out a low whistle. "Impressions of the team?"

"I met one of the four last night—Vince Beck. He seems pretty set in his ways, but he'll have to follow what the owner decides. I'll work on setting up a meeting with her—the name's Stella Cambridge."

Roman handed them each a formal printout of his security proposal. "We'll need to offer a free consult, and I'm willing to extend a significant discount, but we can't implement any of this if we don't get the owner on board."

Hunter glanced at the line items, nodding in agreement at Roman's tentative outline. It was a modest plan that wouldn't come across as too invasive. Two Shield agents on the property—one on day shift, one on night shift in addition to the current setup. New visitor check-in procedures. Upgraded security monitors, locks and key cards. More cameras throughout the property.

"I'd like to put more people here, but we're pretty short-staffed right now, unfortunately," Roman continued. "I'm in the process of interviewing, but new hires will still need training."

"I don't mind switching my shift location for a while." The words came out before Hunter had even thought them through, and Roman and Luke both stared at him.

"That's quite a drive," Luke pointed out.

It was. It would add almost a half hour to his current commute, and he'd be much farther from Josie's school and Levi's day care.

"But it would be temporary," Roman said thoughtfully. "It'd be easier to put a new guy at the Harper estate than to get him trained well enough to set him at Harmony."

Hunter had been working the day shift at the Harper estate for over a year now, an easy gig since Judge William Harper's daughter Natalie had married Luke and was no longer in danger. The property also happened to be just five miles from Hunter's house, which was extremely convenient. But Triss's safety was a sudden priority, and even though he might regret putting himself in a position to spend more time with her, he couldn't seem to convince himself to back off.

"I'm fine with it," he said, and Roman nodded.

"Okay, good. At least for a couple of weeks. Hopefully, we can get things sorted out here quickly and add to our ranks some seasoned guys I'd feel comfortable putting anywhere. I'll think about who to put on night shift. When can we schedule the meeting with Stella?"

"I'm not sure yet. Give me the day. I want to go over and check out Triss's apartment if I can get in there. I was talking to the activities director yesterday about bringing my kids for a visit. Maybe I'll bring them by this afternoon, network a little."

"Network with the elderly?" Luke asked with a hint of skepticism.

Hunter laughed. "Maybe networking isn't the right word."

"I think it's a good idea," Roman said in all seriousness. "Connect with some of the residents and staff first. Show they can trust you. You'll also get more of a feel for what we need there."

A cell-phone alarm started ringing, and Roman pulled out his phone and shut it off.

"Staff prayer. Join me?"

Luke agreed, but Hunter stood to leave. "I'm heading out. I'll touch base tonight."

He waved goodbye and left the room. He'd witnessed the daily staff prayer countless times, but he'd never participated, and he never would. Every morning at shift change, a rotating staff member led a conference call prayer over their clients and their mission. Hunter respected the ritual, but he couldn't buy into it. The safety of their clients was dependent on the team's training, knowledge and strategies. Did he believe that God had a place in there somewhere? Sure, though he was a little gray on exactly where. As far as Hunter was concerned, he had a job to do. Security at Harmony was now his responsibility. God knew what they needed, but if they failed, it was on them. Just like Viv's death was on him. God had known Vivian needed to get to the hospital. Hunter had failed to act. That was on him, and he'd spend the rest of his life making sure he never failed to act again.

A few hours after leaving the hospital, Hunter stood in the center of Triss's charred apartment and turned in a slow circle, his gaze touching every square inch. The fire had swept quickly out of the kitchen and partially into the living room. The bookshelves and their contents—rubble. The couches, scorched and irreparable. The curtains, mere remnants. The only items in the living room that had escaped total destruction were the glass-and-iron coffee table, the leather recliner, the wall-mounted television and a mammoth chest behind the couch near the far wall.

It was hard to believe all this damage had started with a rag on the stove. He looked up at the ceiling, noted the smoke detectors. Wouldn't they have picked up the fire before it had gotten so out of control?

If Triss was right and someone had purposely started

the fire, had that same someone done something to render her unconscious? Hoped she'd wake too late, if at all?

He picked his way across the living room to the adjoining kitchen. The space was no more than a hundred square feet, the formerly white cabinets scorched black, the white fridge a sooty gray, the microwave melted above what was left of the oven. He stepped into the space, careful not to touch anything. Technically, he shouldn't be in here, but no one had kept him out, and it had been easy to pry open the loosely tacked-on piece of drywall that had replaced the apartment door after the investigators finally left a while ago. He stared at the blackened stovetop, the knobs melted beyond recognition. If there were clues to be found, he didn't see any. He'd want to speak with the fire inspector later.

Turning out of the kitchen, he pushed open the door to Triss's bedroom. Nothing seemed amiss there, except for the blackened wall that adjoined the kitchen and the thick odor of smoke. He coughed and cleared his throat, realizing he shouldn't stick around much longer without a mask.

But as he returned to the living room, his attention caught again on the chest by the couch. Idly, he lifted the hinged cover and was surprised to find the items inside protected from the fire.

But before letting the lid drop, he took a closer look at the contents and paused. His heartbeat quickened as he kneeled next to the chest to get a closer look. A lilac baby onesie with the price tag still attached. A board book with textures. He gently pushed the items aside, knowing he shouldn't be looking through Triss's things, but compelled. A plush teddy bear with a pacifier. A dollhouse with a miniature family set. And a lifelike doll with light tan skin and pitch-black curls.

Hunter didn't know what he was looking at, but he knew it was none of his business to be looking at it. He was closing the lid on the chest when a gasp sounded behind him.

He turned his head, embarrassed and guilty to see Triss standing in the entryway, a mix of shock and anger darkening her eyes.

"What are you doing?" Triss's heart was thumping wildly—she was horrified to find Hunter digging through her personal things. Even more horrified at what he'd found. No one had ever seen the items before. *No one.*

He let the lid of the chest snap closed. "Sorry." He stood, shoving his hands in the pockets of his black dress pants, and Triss told herself not to notice the way his white button-down fitted to his chest under his tailored suit jacket, the way his presence filled the entire apartment, the sincerity in his expression. "I wanted to take a look around, get a feel for what happened. See if anything made it through the fire."

Triss scanned the room quickly, realizing that not much had made it through, and she wanted to weep with the realization that the gifts had been protected. But she also wanted Hunter out. Because she didn't want to answer the question in his eyes.

He moved toward her, and she realized that her breathing was uneven. Her chest was rising and falling rapidly, and it wasn't just because Hunter had seen the evidence. It was because of Hunter's presence itself.

He stopped a foot in front of her, and he waited a beat, as if seeing if she would volunteer any information. Finally, he said, "I talked to Roman and Luke this morning."

"I know," Triss said before he could say more. "They told me you volunteered to take on the day shift here. But don't."

"Don't?"

"It doesn't make any sense. Your kids' schools are too far. You're a single parent. You don't need that commute. Someone else can do it."

For a moment, he was silent, and Triss was sure he could hear the beat of her heart. It was such a rebel, her heart. Somehow, it knew all that she wanted and didn't deserve. All that she longed for but would never have. In the months since she'd separated herself from Hunter and his kids, she'd focused all her energies into the people at Harmony and her studies at school, actively rejecting the traitorous pull of her heart.

And now, here he was again, staring into her eyes with a warmth that she'd spent months convincing herself she could live without.

"Too late."

"Excuse me?"

"I already said I'd do it. I'm not backing out." He grinned, and his dimples destroyed the last of her defenses.

Triss's lips twitched, despite herself. Every time she took herself too seriously, he made her want to smile.

She crossed her arms, fighting the urge. "Okay, boss," she said, attempting a casual tone, as if she was unfazed by the idea of daily contact with Hunter. "What's the plan, then?"

"Samantha's breaking my kids out of school and day care in a couple of hours and bringing them here for some Play-Doh action. Thought it'd be a way to get to know some of the residents and staff. Maybe blend in as a friend for a while before breaking out the security hat."

Play-Doh. If it was possible for a heart to melt to the floor, that's what Triss's did as she imagined Hunter facilitating a Play-Doh extravaganza with the residents and his two adorable kids. "Sounds like a blast," she said noncommittally.

He followed her into the hallway and tacked the drywall board over the door. "Where will you sleep tonight?"

"Stella's getting one of the other apartments ready. She said I can move in after lunch."

"I can help you bring over what's salvageable."

"I don't think I'll take much. The smoke did a lot of damage."

"You'll need some new things."

"The apartment she's getting ready comes furnished, but I'll need new clothes. I'll probably go out tonight after dinner."

"Bryan's on night shift. Make sure he goes with you."

"Something tells me I wouldn't be able to stop him if I tried."

"True." A pause. Then he added, "I was surprised to see you here so early."

Obviously. "There was no other reason to keep me. The doctor said they'd call when the rest of the test results come in."

"Where are we headed?" he asked as she led the way down the hall and through the common area.

"Chair-fit."

"Chair what?"

"Fit." She gave him the side-eye, glancing at his attire.

"If you want to blend in, you'll want to rethink your uniform. Not to mention, chair-fit is hard to do in a suit."

She walked through an open doorway into a studio with hardwood floors and floor-to-ceiling mirrors, a dozen chairs in two staggered rows.

She glanced at her watch. "We have about ten minutes, but everyone will start trickling in soon. Help me get things set up?"

He followed her dutifully, setting out five-pound weights, resistance bands and balance balls. She tried her best to ignore him. It was impossible.

She was never so relieved when Sissy Maynard showed up. Triss was convinced that Sissy's name was code for Sassy because the woman was a fireball of energy and borderline inappropriate humor. Her short hair was faintly blue today, courtesy, no doubt, of her latest boxed dye.

"Oooh, la la!" Sissy exclaimed as she entered the fitness room and cast her eyes on Hunter. She feathered a hand through her wispy hair. "No one told me we had a new instructor."

Triss snorted. "Don't get your hopes up, Sissy. Courtney will be here like she always is. This is my friend Hunter. He forgot to dress down."

"You'll want to lose that jacket and tie, honey," Sissy said, glancing at her black leotard–clad figure in the mirrors. "Where are you sitting?"

"Next to you, of course," he answered, and Triss heard the smile in his voice. Against her better judgment, she glanced up and caught his expression in the mirror. His broad grin, those dimples... He winked, and her heart dipped. Stupid heart.

It wasn't long before the rest of the class and Courtney arrived. Hunter tossed his jacket and tie on an empty chair, rolled up his sleeves and took his place next to Sissy like the good sport he was.

"You don't have to do it," Triss said quietly. "I do a little and walk around and help encourage everyone."

"I don't mind," he said.

The music started, and Courtney's peppy voice filled the small room. "Let's warm up!" she yelled.

"I'm already warm!" Sissy yelled back. "I'm sitting next to Mr. Muscles."

The group laughed, and Triss couldn't help but join in. He did have some serious muscles, one of his many attractive qualities.

"There's an empty seat next to me, Mr. Muscles," Iris Patterson called out, her smooth British accent making the quip all the funnier. "That will *certainly* keep me awake!"

Triss rolled her eyes. As long as she remembered to take her medicine for narcolepsy, Iris overflowed with flirtatious humor.

Leading the class, Courtney Tompkins, the nursing-school grad student everyone went to with aches and pains, was energetic and smiley, but Triss knew the pain she was hiding. Her grandfather, Walter, had been the first of the four recent deaths, and the two had been close. Come to think of it, Courtney had been quiet at Triss's security meeting the other day. Maybe she could pull her aside later and have a chat. Chances were pretty high that Courtney was on board with the security plans but didn't have the gumption to voice her opinion in the face of all the naysayers.

They were twenty minutes into the class when Triss's cell phone vibrated. She glanced at it and saw it was the hospital. Waving the phone toward Hunter, she stepped into the hallway to answer.

"Is this Triss Everett?"

"Yes."

"Hi, Triss, this is Dr. O'Neill. I'm calling with test results. Your toxicology report showed the presence of sodium oxybate." He paused as if she might see the significance, but then continued. "You take no daily medications, correct?"

"Right."

"That rules out Xyrem," he said quietly, and Triss tried to follow the explanation.

"You may have heard of GHB," he said then. "Looks like you may have been the victim of the date-rape drug."

Triss straightened. "What? How?"

Hunter appeared at her side and stayed as she listened to the advice of the doctor to report the incident to the police, and to review all that had happened the night before to try to figure out how she had ingested the drug. Finally, she disconnected the call, her mind tracing back to yesterday evening, as faces and conversations flashed through her memory.

"You're shaking." Hunter set his hand on her arm, as if to anchor her, but she pulled away and stepped back. His touch was too intimate, breaching all the boundaries she'd drawn. She needed to think.

"Toxicology report showed possible GHB," she told him, struggling to make sense of what was going on. Maybe the car accident and the apartment fire could be explained away, but this couldn't. "Someone drugged me."

FIVE

The toxicology report changed everything. Officer Goodson and his partner, Nicole Quinn, were on-site within an hour, scanning the visitor log from yesterday and interviewing residents and staff. Tensions were high as the Harmony community whispered and speculated about what, exactly, the police could be looking for. Officer Goodson had advised Triss not to discuss what had happened until after he'd interviewed everyone, and that only contributed to her growing unease. If there was a killer in their midst, she wanted to warn her friends.

Of course, if there was a killer in their midst, then there was a high possibility that the killer actually *was* one of her friends. The thought sat in the pit of her stomach like a massive stone as she tried to stay out of the way and avoid conversation.

And then, Levi and Josie arrived with a giant bucket of Play-Doh. At two and five—nearly six, as Josie was quick to remind her—they were just what everyone needed to lighten the dark mood.

"Twiss!" Levi shrieked as he toddled forward and

tripped over his tiny feet, his knees hitting tile for a fraction of a second before he pushed himself up and kept running.

Triss crouched and braced herself for his trademark running leap, and he didn't disappoint as he launched himself into her arms, his chubby ones wrapping around her.

His ruffled hair tickled her chin, and she thought she detected the scent of Oreos, his favorite snack.

"Hey, buddy," she whispered, and then started to set him down, but he held on tight and Josie appeared next to them. She wore her hair in long brown pigtails, her edges curling up around her face as she clutched the large bucket of Play-Doh to her chest, a serious expression on her face.

"Hi, Triss," she said, her voice solemn. "Are you doing Play-Doh with us?"

The last thing Triss wanted to do was play with these two kids who had wedged their way into her heart, but she couldn't say no. Not with Josie staring seriously at her, a challenge in her eyes. It was as if she was saying "Where have you been?"

"Sure. I can play for a little while," she said, starting to stand, but Levi wouldn't loosen his hold.

She shifted his body weight in her arms, then stood. "We're going to play in this big room over here." She led the way, Levi's fingers pinching the skin at her nape.

"Who do we have here?" George Wyrick asked, looking up from his book with an interested smile.

Josie walked right up to him. "I'm Josie," she said. "What's your name?"

"Well, hello, Josie. I'm George. Pleased to meet you."

"Do you wanna do Play-Doh with us?"

George set his book on the side table and pushed down the footrest on his recliner. "I don't think I've touched the stuff in fifty years. That sounds like fun."

"It is!" Levi exclaimed, wiggling from Triss's arms and toddling over to the table where Hunter had set the bucket. He climbed onto a chair and threw the top half of his body on the bucket, yanking hard at the lid.

"Here, big guy." Hunter reached over and pried off the lid, then pushed the bucket over to the kids. Josie and Levi both grabbed armfuls of smaller containers and started handing them to the residents.

"Oh, my, how adorable," Kaye said as she entered the room, her expression bright. "Josie and Levi, right?"

Josie nodded with a shy smile and handed a container of Play-Doh to Kaye.

"Look at this, Iris!" George hollered across the room.

Iris glanced up from her solitaire game on a computer. "I'll be right there. Save me a blue."

"How about you, Don?" Triss called. Donald Keaton had positioned himself at a computer in the corner of the room. He peeked over the computer monitor, shook his nearly bald head briskly and returned to whatever he was doing. A heavy sadness yanked on Triss's heart. Two days before Genevieve died, Don had bought an engagement ring for her. The student residents and staff had all been working together to help him plan a romantic proposal evening. Since Genevieve's death, Don had barely come out of his room, and when he did, he made it clear he didn't want to have any conversations.

"Play-Doh!" Riley's tinny voice sounded from the hall, and Triss bristled. Everything about the girl rubbed her wrong. Riley bustled into the room and grabbed a black, yanking off the lid and rolling the dough into a ball. "We used to play this game—everyone had to, like, make something based on a theme, and then the others tried to guess it."

"That sounds fun," said Josie, who was busy making a purple flower. "What's a theme?"

"Like, you know, we would all make an animal, or we would all make a dessert," Riley said, flashing a bright smile at Josie. She wore too much makeup, but she still only ever looked about twelve years old, and Triss wondered how she'd do in her upcoming law-firm internship.

"Next week's Thanksgiving," Kaye said. "How about everyone makes something related to Thanksgiving?"

"Or Cwismiss!" Levi shouted.

"Christmas would be easier," Hunter agreed with a laugh.

"Well, look at this," the activities director said, sweeping into the room with a pleased smile. What had started as four or five residents in the room had quickly morphed into a packed room of seniors making shapes with the Play-Doh. Even some of the staff had started to get into it. "Now that I know what a hit a kid's toy can be, I may just spend a little less time planning all of these elaborate activities around here," Brandon said.

"Oh, no, you don't," Kaye said. "I've been looking forward to tomorrow's cruise for almost a month now."

"Cruise?" Hunter asked close to Triss's ear, and she

rejected the spiral of warmth that flooded her veins at his nearness.

She walked around the table to reach a container of green.

"Tomorrow, a small group is going on a little lunch cruise at the Inner Harbor." She rolled the green into a cone shape and started pinching the edges to make a Christmas tree.

"You going, or do you have class?" Hunter had followed her closely, his own hands idly rolling a lump of orange.

"I'm going. Classes are Monday through Thursday mornings for me. I missed today." She wasn't too worried about it. They were off next week for Thanksgiving, and her instructor said she'd post the notes online.

"I made a stocking!" Levi announced.

"Matches my hair," Kaye said with a laugh. "Here, what do you think I'm working on?" She pointed to the table, where she had set three small round balls, one on top of the other.

"Fwosty!"

Kaye laughed, clearly delighted. "That's right. What else does Frosty the Snowman need?"

"Cowitt nose!"

"Yes, a carrot nose! Who has orange?"

"Heads up!" Hunter called, and tossed a small bit of orange into his son's hands. Then he leaned closer to Triss. "I know I should be correcting those *R*s, but I can't bring myself to."

"He'll outgrow it, and you'll miss it," Triss pointed out. As if she had any business giving parenting advice.

She rounded the table again to get some more space between them, grabbing another container of Play-Doh.

"Purple for a Christmas tree?" Hunter asked, and when she looked up and met his eyes, she saw him trying to read her.

Triss looked at the purple she'd absently picked up, then pulled off a tiny piece and rolled it into a ball. "Ornaments."

"Creative," Hunter said, amusement lighting his eyes. This time, he didn't follow her. Instead, his gaze roamed the room, and she could see that work mode was kicking in as Zach walked in with Courtney. The two had been dating almost since they'd first moved to Harmony in August, and nearly always showed up as a pair.

Triss introduced the two to Hunter as Officer Goodson and his partner made their way into the room.

"We're heading out," Officer Goodson said. "We'll be in touch."

Triss thanked them both, swallowing her frustration. She knew they couldn't discuss their findings with her, but time wasn't exactly on their side and she wanted to know everything the police knew.

Kaye appeared at Triss's side, her eyes troubled as she absently rolled a white ball of Play-Doh in her palms. "You already had me a little worried, but with the police coming around now…"

"I think the police are here out of an abundance of caution, Kaye," Zach volunteered, his voice reassuring. "Any fire needs to be investigated."

"They weren't just asking about the fire, though," Kaye pointed out.

"What else were they asking about?" Hunter asked, and Triss knew he asked the question only to get conversation flowing, to see if he could glean any more clues.

"Everything," Courtney answered, rubbing her hands along her arms as if to ward off a sudden chill.

"Not just about last night with the fire, but about the deaths, too," Zach said, rubbing Courtney's back. "You okay?"

"It's hard," Courtney said, her blue eyes brimming with tears. "I get it that they need to investigate, but I don't think Gramps's death is part of any of it."

"Your grandfather was Walter, right?" Hunter asked, and Courtney nodded.

"We'd been talking about moving him to Silverwood. His memory was going." Her bottom lip trembled and she pressed her mouth closed. She cleared her throat. "I think he overdosed by accident with the insulin."

"Because of the memory problems?" Hunter asked gently.

She swiped at a tear that flew down her cheek, then tried on a wobbly smile. "He didn't want to move to Silverwood, though. I know that much. I hate that he's gone, but it's probably better this way." She shrugged. "At least, that's what I try to tell myself."

"I think you're right," Kristy Ingles said, appearing in the doorway. The other graduate student resident at Harmony, she was pursuing a psychology career, and could always be counted on for the right words at the right time. "Loss is painful no matter what," she said, her dark eyes full of sympathy. "But it's incredibly painful to watch the people we love deteriorate."

Courtney nodded. "Exactly."

"So true," Kaye said, passing a container of yellow to Kristy. "Play-Doh?"

Kristy smiled widely, bronze lipstick highlighting a perfect white smile on midnight skin.

"Don't mind if I do," she said with good humor.

Kaye didn't acknowledge Zach and Courtney, and Triss wondered if she was holding last night against Zach. She'd spoken to Kaye earlier, and had listened as she recounted all the details of the night before, and how Zach didn't think she should call 911. Whatever Kaye's judgment, Triss thought nothing of Zach's reluctance to call 911. He seemed to be a bright and clearheaded kind of guy. He'd probably assumed Kaye was overreacting, which was a logical assumption.

As Triss observed Hunter making conversation and getting to know the people at Harmony, she could almost see him committing names and details to memory. Some residents stayed for a while, and others just passed through with quick smiles. Eventually, though, the hour grew late and people started trickling back to their rooms or the dining hall.

Triss observed silently, her gaze touching on each person who entered and left. She wondered if any of them had it in them to kill. Surely not grieving Don, settled into the computer in the corner. Or Sissy with her jokes and her blue hair, or Kaye with her vivacious personality. George was known to save spiders that happened into the facility, and his buddy Mack was just as harmless. Her gaze touched on her fellow graduate students, but didn't stay long there, either. Zach was going into sports medicine with a minor in music and was known for giving impromptu guitar and voice concerts before dinner. His girlfriend, Courtney, the resident nurse and germaphobe, was now bustling around the room spritzing tables with cleanser and wiping them down—something she did often when she wasn't interviewing residents for her graduate project on loneliness and the elderly. Riley didn't seem sophisticated enough to pull off a killing spree, and Kristy was one of the friendliest people Triss had ever met. That left several residents Triss didn't know well, and the staff—the security team, the chef, the housekeepers. Not to mention all the people who lived at the other two facilities, plus many random visitors, though outside involvement seemed unlikely at this point.

"Josie, Levi, time to start cleaning up," Hunter said, pulling Triss from her thoughts. "You eating in the dining hall?" he asked her. "Samantha packed dinner for the kids."

"I usually do," Triss said, scouring her brain for any excuse to eat alone in her new apartment. But she had no food in her kitchen yet, and Hunter knew it. She shoved more Play-Doh into a container and snapped on a lid.

She wasn't surprised by her conflicting emotions. She'd recognized them for what they were earlier this summer. As much as she loved being around Hunter and his kids, they weren't good for her. She'd worked hard to focus on her goals and not allow anything to sidetrack her. And she'd done such a good job of it that she had almost convinced herself that she'd imagined her feelings for Hunter and been confused by her attachment to his kids. Today, in one short hour, she'd been blind-sided by the depth of her feelings for them. *Not good*.

It could never work, and she knew it. Secrets de-stroyed relationships. And she was harboring a secret that she could never tell Hunter, or anyone, about.

"Can you do this every Thursday?" Brandon asked, passing Hunter a handful of Play-Doh containers.

"No," Triss said automatically, and both men looked up at her in surprise. She was immediately embarrassed by how adamant she'd sounded. "They don't live close," she explained, "and Josie had to leave school early to get here before dinner."

"We could come on some holidays, though, or Sat-urdays," Hunter offered.

"Not this Saturday, though! It's my birthday!" Josie announced with a little bounce in her step as she toted two more containers over and dropped them in the bucket.

"How old will you be?" Brandon asked.

Six, Triss thought before Josie said the number out loud. Six beautiful, adorable, love-filled years old.

"Six!" Josie said, and then her attention flew to Triss as if she'd just remembered something. She ran around the table and up to her dad, tapping him on the arm and tugging him to her level. She stood on tiptoe and whis-pered something in his ear. Hunter hesitated for a bare second, but nodded, his expression giving nothing away.

Josie bounced away from him and raced up to Triss. "I'm having a zoo birthday! Dad said you can come, too!"

Her sweet voice wrapped around Triss's heart and squeezed. No, she couldn't go to the birthday party at the zoo with Hunter's perfect little girl. She couldn't possibly go. Not when she had missed her own daughter's birthday party every year for the past five years. Not when, in two short weeks, she'd miss the sixth one. But Josie's eyes were fixed on her with hope, and she couldn't think of an excuse. So even though her heart said no, she said, "That sounds like a lot of fun."

But it didn't. Even as Josie spun around with a happy shout and Triss tried to tell herself it was not a big deal, conflicting feelings of guilt and love rose up and overwhelmed her.

"Great. It's at one. We'll pick you up at twelve," Hunter said, his eyes scanning her face, as if he could read her thoughts.

She focused on pressing the ill-fitting lid back on the bucket, willing away the sudden sting in her eyes.

"Everything okay?" Hunter's hand came to her shoulder. She let go of the container and whirled away from his touch, rejecting the warmth that coursed through her.

"Sorry, I—" he began.

"I can't get that lid on," Triss said quickly, heart thumping wildly as she gestured to the bucket as if she'd given up on an impossible challenge.

Hunter stared at her for a half second, but then reached out and pressed the lid onto the bucket without saying a word.

Heat crept up Triss's neck at her jumpy response to him. Something had happened yesterday when he'd pulled her out of the car, and when he'd lifted her into his arms. Triss had always been careful to avoid his touch until yesterday. Now, it seemed like he was everywhere. She could still feel his steady grip on her as he'd toted her to the car, the beat of his heart under her ear. And now, every touch was magnified. She suspected he felt it, too.

"Daddy, I'm hungwy," Levi said, popping a thumb in his mouth, his raven hair spiking in too many directions.

"We're eating now, buddy," Hunter assured him. "Follow Triss."

It was another half hour before Hunter's shift would be over. Dinner wouldn't kill her. She led the way to the dining room, the scent of pasta making her stomach rumble. Had she even eaten today?

Triss pointed to a long table by the windows where people were already seated. "You can set the kids up there," she said. "I'll get you a plate."

Hunter waved her off, leading his kids to the table. "I'll eat at home."

Triss sidestepped the buffet Barb had set up with baked ziti, salad and rolls, making her way directly to the kitchen to pull one of the premade meals from the fridge.

"Oh, Triss, I've got a hot dish for you," Barb said before Triss had even made it to the fridge. "Just a minute." She finished washing a pot and set it on the drying rack, then pulled on a mitt and reached into the oven. She took out a small square glass dish with what looked like baked ziti.

"Dairy-free baked ziti?" Triss asked, barely hiding her excitement.

Barb grinned proudly. "If you're willing to try some cheese substitutes I've been experimenting with."

Triss wasn't picky—never had been. "I'll try any-thing once."

Barb dished a serving onto a plate. "I'll put the rest in some individual containers and pop them in the freezer for another day."

"You're amazing," Triss said. "Thank you."

She walked into the dining hall, dropped two rolls on her plate and made her way to the now nearly full table where Hunter and the kids had set up. Hunter had saved a spot next to him, and Triss was almost too hungry to even think about his physical proximity to her. But no sooner had she sat and pulled out her fork than Iris gasped loudly, her plate clattering to the floor.

"Oh, I've gone and made a mess!" She scooted back from the table, red pasta falling off her lap and onto the floor.

Next to her, Courtney and Zach jumped into action, reaching for napkins, and Triss hurried over to help as well. Luke appeared at her side, using napkins to scoop ziti into a trash can Kristy had dragged over.

As they cleaned up the last of it, a housekeeper appeared with a mop, and Iris excused herself to go change.

Triss made her way to her seat, feeling a little sorry for Iris and how embarrassed she'd seemed. She won-dered if she'd started to fall asleep and had knocked over her food. Occasionally, she forgot to take her medi-cation, and she'd fall asleep in the middle of a conver-sation.

She pulled her chair in and took a bite of the baked ziti Barb had prepared for her. Amazing. The woman was a genius. She took another bite, considering the idea of asking Barb to go ahead and leave another serving in the fridge because she'd want it for lunch the next day. But then her throat suddenly felt itchy.

She set down her fork and grabbed her water, drinking quickly with the false hope that this was not an allergic reaction.

But it was, and it came on quick, the skin around her mouth tingling and a cough coming on.

"Are you okay?" Hunter turned to her, alarm in his expression.

She was coughing too hard to answer, the coughs ending in a wheeze more painful than she'd ever experienced. Her pulse skyrocketed, fear closing in as her airway constricted.

"Your EpiPen," Hunter said urgently, immediately assessing the problem. "Where is it?"

It was in her school backpack, but she couldn't get the words out.

Around her, people were jumping into action, and Triss saw Barb running to the table, panic written all over her face.

"No!" she cried. "I was careful. I was—" Her hands came to her mouth in horror.

"Kaye, call 911!" Hunter shouted, thrusting his phone at her. Then he passed a key to Kristy as he pulled Triss out of her chair. "Zach, Courtney, Kristy—ransack her apartment and find that EpiPen!"

Hunter carefully moved Triss to the floor, where someone had tossed a thick red crocheted blanket.

Her dark eyes were wide with panic as she struggled to breathe, pink hives spreading fast from her neck to her chest. "Help is on the way," Hunter said, wrapping a hand around hers and trying to keep his voice steady. "They'll find the EpiPen."

"Will this help?" George asked, and he handed over a travel-sized bottle of Benadryl.

Triss reached for it, nodding. Hunter grabbed it, pulled off the lid and fished out two pills as someone pressed a cup of water toward Triss.

She was wheezing more than coughing now, and he wasn't sure she could even swallow the pills, but he lifted her head and she managed to down the two pills and a couple of swigs of water.

"My backpack," she choked out, before another cough took hold.

"The EpiPen?"

She nodded weakly.

"I'll tell them!" Barb said, and took off running.

Long seconds passed as Triss's wheezing grew louder, and then Josie appeared at his side, her brown eyes filled with tears, her nose pink.

"Daddy, what's wrong with Triss?" she asked.

Levi sat frozen in his seat at the table, thumb in his mouth.

"She's going to be okay," he said, hoping he was telling the truth. "She's allergic to something she ate."

"What's 'allergic'?"

"Here!" Kristy yelled, rushing toward them with the EpiPen. She skidded to a stop and dropped to the floor next to Triss, whose labored breaths were echoing through the silent dining hall.

"What do I do?"

Courtney was steps behind her. She kneeled next to Triss, grabbed the EpiPen from Kristy and thrust the orange tip against Triss's right thigh, holding it in place. Hunter could do nothing but hold Triss's hand. He locked eyes with her, willing the medicine to do its job. He knew that sometimes, it was too little, too late.

The room was silent and everyone was on their feet with worry, the only sound Triss's labored breathing. And then she gasped, one big breath, then again, and a glint of relief filled her eyes. Sirens sounded nearby, and Hunter felt Triss squeeze his hand. She was not going to be victim number five. Not tonight. Not ever, if he had a say in the matter. He ran a shaky hand through his hair, his attention lighting on Barb, who was standing worriedly near the kitchen. What had gone wrong with dinner? Certainly she knew about Triss's allergy. And what was Triss thinking—eating baked ziti despite her dairy allergy?

As the paramedics arrived, Hunter retreated to give them room to work, then turned to find the kids. They were standing by the table, Josie holding Levi's hand tightly, Levi's thumb in his mouth. His heart swelled at the sight. He hoped they always had such a strong bond. As an only child, that was something he'd missed out on. He crouched to pull them both into a hug.

"Is she gonna be okay?" Josie asked, her delicate eyebrows furrowed.

"Yes." His throat was tight as he hugged his daughter and remembered the night she'd finally understood her mother was never coming back. "She's going to be fine," he whispered.

"What's going on?" a voice asked behind him, and Hunter turned to see Bryan in the entrance to the dining hall.

"You're early."

Bryan scanned the chaotic room, the paramedics loading Triss onto a stretcher. "Looks like I'm late."

Hunter explained what had happened, his attention flickering to Barb. Her eyes were glossy as she stood at the counter, her face as white as the fridge behind her.

"Can we go home, Daddy?" Josie asked.

He didn't want to go home. He wanted to stay and see what Barb had to say, make sure Triss was okay. But Bryan was here and could ask Barb the questions. Not to mention, Hunter could already hear Triss telling the paramedics she was fine now. His kids were hungry and tired and probably a little traumatized. He had to go.

"Sure, Josie-bug, let me just say goodbye to Triss."

He approached Triss as the paramedics wheeled the stretcher down a ramp and out of Creekside. The hives were already fading, and her breathing was under control. She was using her quick recovery to her advantage and trying to convince the paramedics she was fine.

"You need to get checked out," Hunter interrupted, and she speared him with a look of frustration. "You can't mess with an allergy like this. Especially considering what happened yesterday."

The fight seemed to go out of her. "You're right," she said softly.

"I'm calling Luke to meet you up there."

"Please don't. He worries enough."

"He'll kill me if I don't."

"True."

"I can follow you there if you want—"

"No." Her tone was adamant. "Take the kids home," she added more gently, her gaze dropping to her hands.

If he didn't have the kids with him, nothing could have kept him from going to the hospital with her, but he could see she was determined to keep him away. She'd made every effort to distance herself from him earlier, during the activity, and she'd practically leaped across the room when he'd lightly touched her. He reminded himself that she had dropped out of his life and the kids' lives for a reason, and he'd respect her choice even if he didn't understand it. He'd volunteered to spend the next week here, at least, and his responsibility was to protect her—not get sidelined by an attraction that had no place here and was clearly unreciprocated.

"I'm calling Officer Goodson on my way home," he said as the paramedics maneuvered the stretcher into the ambulance.

"It was an accident," Triss said. "Barb will explain."

The doors shut and Hunter returned to Creekside. He found it hard to believe it was an accident, but Triss had seemed convinced. He'd call Officer Goodson, anyway, just to be on the safe side. He said goodbye to Bryan and led the kids to the common area. Josie ran to grab the bucket of Play-Doh, and as she was lifting it off the table, it dropped, the lid popping off and containers rolling in every direction.

The kids laughed and started chasing the containers. Hunter suppressed a sigh and followed along. A tub of yellow rolled toward the computer niche, and then made its way under the desks to the back of the room. Hunter jogged in that direction but the container rolled under the desks before he could catch it. He went around the row to grab it and accidentally startled Donald Keaton, who was still at the corner computer after all this time. The man had been slumped so low in his seat that Hunter hadn't realized he was still there. Don jumped slightly, and Hunter noticed the quick blink of the computer screen. He'd minimized the browser window he'd been on, and now an empty Google search page was open.

"Didn't mean to startle you," Hunter said, picking up the container casually.

Don blinked, appearing sleepy. "I guess I dozed for a bit."

"Dinner's still going, if you're hungry."

Don stood. "I think I am."

Had he really slept through the paramedics arriving? And what had he been doing on the computer that he'd wanted to hide? Hunter didn't know much about computers himself, but he knew someone who did. He'd put a call in to Harrison, the college computer whiz Shield sometimes contracted out, see if he could do a little unofficial search of Harmony's public computers. Hunter filed away the thought and said good-night, then gathered the kids and headed to the car.

The wind was whipping outside, leaves flying around

the parking lot as Josie buckled in and Hunter snapped Levi's car seat buckles.

"Can we have hot chocolate for dessert?" Josie asked.

"We'll see," Hunter replied, but his mind wasn't on the kids or the pretty fall leaves or hot chocolate. He shut the door of his truck and took a long look at the property. What was happening at Harmony? Was there a killer on-site? A resident? A staff member? One of the graduate students?

He got in his truck and turned it on. One Shield agent was not enough. Tomorrow, he'd go hard on Stella and try to convince her to agree to more. And he'd offer to help Roman conduct some interviews and do some training. He trusted Bryan, but there was a reason Shield operated almost exclusively in teams. And with Triss's life on the line, Hunter refused to take any unnecessary risks.

SIX

"This is overkill." Stella handed Roman's proposal back to him, her voice flat. But Hunter read uncertainty in her eyes. He and Roman had presented her with enough evidence to make her question whether Harmony's current security protocols were enough.

"It's temporary," Hunter reminded her.

"And if investigations continue to go the way we think they're going, police will start looking into the four recent deaths here pretty soon," Roman added, his dark gray eyes serious. "If that happens, you'll have a lot of concerned family calling and asking you what you're doing to keep their loved ones safe."

Hunter could almost see the shift in Stella's perspective at that line of reasoning. She might not like to be told what to do, but she was a smart woman. Most of Harmony's residents were relatively wealthy, and the community had an unblemished reputation. If she wanted to stay in business, she needed to at least go through the motions of making it appear that she was taking a vested interest in the safety of her residents.

"I don't have the budget for it," she finally said.

"Cut the budget somewhere else," Roman suggested, clearly not buying her excuse. "The biggest cost is up front for the equipment. I'm giving you a massive break on the manpower and labor."

"And once all this mess is sorted out, you can decide whether or not to keep agents on the ground or to stick with your own private security company and simply use the equipment and protocols we set up," Hunter added.

Roman passed her the paper again, and she reluctantly accepted it, then sighed.

"I can't pay for more agents," she finally said. "You'll have to work with your two guys for now, and get my guys on board with your plan."

"We can work with that," Roman said. "You're making a good decision."

He pulled out a contract from his briefcase and nodded to Hunter. That was his cue. Hunter excused himself and went directly to his truck to start transporting the equipment he'd be installing. He'd get Adam and Vince on board early, and they could keep working when he went on the lunch cruise in a couple of hours.

His first order of business would be installing the security cameras throughout the grounds. If they'd had one in the dining hall yesterday, they would have had a clear picture of what had happened at dinner.

He took the dolly out of his truck and started loading it up, thinking over what Bryan had told him after his conversation with Barb. Barb had insisted she'd been meticulous about her ingredients, and she'd served Triss her meal personally. It was possible that Triss was allergic to one of the cheese substitutes Barb had used, but unlikely. Hunter finished loading the equipment and locked up his truck, then pushed the dolly across the parking lot toward Creekside, thinking over the events of the night for the thousandth time. He kept coming back to Iris's accident with the pasta. It was the only time Triss had left her food. Had someone switched her plate in all the commotion? The dishes had long since been cleaned up, and without cameras, there was no way to know if his theory was correct. But they did have the rest of the ziti Barb had made for Triss, and they had an ingredients list. Triss could at least undergo allergy testing to rule out the possibility that Barb's experimental meal had accidentally caused anaphylaxis.

As he approached the entrance to Creekside, Kaye opened the door for him. The mood seemed somber inside—several residents were reading in chairs in the commons or fiddling with their phones or the computers. He checked his watch. Triss would be out soon. She'd been released from the hospital a couple of hours ago and she'd had to get a school assignment completed and submitted. Despite what she'd gone through, she still intended to go on the lunch cruise today. Hunter was uneasy about the idea, but he was just as uneasy about the idea of letting the group go on the trip with no protection. At least he and Triss would both be there, and they'd both be armed.

He spotted Adam leaning against a far wall, scrolling on his phone. Too distracted for a security officer. Hunter shook off his irritation and called his name, signaling for him to come over. Adam pushed off from the wall and shoved his phone into the pocket of his wrinkly uniform slacks. He pushed his too-long hair out of his eyes and approached Hunter, eyeing the equipment warily.

"I'm no electrician," he said. "You might have the wrong guy for this."

Hunter studied the young man for a moment, gauged him to be around twenty or twenty-one. Tall and gangly, he walked with slightly hunched shoulders and a general lack of confidence. "This doesn't require an electrician," Hunter said, handing Adam a box. "Go ahead and pull out the equipment. I'll teach you how to do it."

"Where are you putting that?" Don asked, looking up from his isolated position behind the computer.

"This one's going right there," Hunter said, pointing to a spot above the entrance to the room. The wide angle of the camera would catch everything—including whatever was on the screens of the row of computers Don was hanging out at. The second one would go in the kitchen, and the third in the dining hall.

As he painstakingly instructed Adam on how to install the first camera, Triss appeared at his side, holding a camera from a box she'd apparently already opened.

He glanced at her, relieved to see no trace of the allergic reaction and that her hives were gone. She wore a pair of dark jeans with a gray, long-sleeve T-shirt, her hair twisted softly away from her face.

"What are you doing?" he asked. "I think the doctor wanted you to be taking it easy."

"I'm not much for lying around," she said. "I'm just observing." She motioned to Adam on the ladder. "Proceed."

Hunter knew what she was doing. She was going to learn by watching, and then she'd run circles around the team installing cameras on her own. He should insist she rest, but he knew that would be futile, and he wanted the cameras up fast. He turned to Adam and continued the installation, aware every second of Triss's presence.

"Wow, you guys aren't messing around."

Hunter turned from the camera to find Riley entering the room. She gaped at the camera they were installing and loudly smacked what must have been several pieces of gum in her mouth.

"Morning, Riley," Hunter said, ignoring her comment.

"Don't you think it'd be better to have, like, spy cameras?" she asked, stepping closer.

"What do you mean?" he asked, glancing at Triss and reading annoyance on her face.

"Like, hidden cameras to catch the bad guy instead of visible cameras the bad guy will avoid."

"Not really expecting to catch a bad guy with the cameras," Hunter said, though he was hoping to catch some clues. "Think of the cameras as a first line of protection. And peace of mind."

Riley snapped her gum and shrugged. "I don't like it. I had more peace of mind when cameras weren't following my every move."

"I'm sure we'll get used to it," Iris said, looking up from her game of solitaire.

"Hey, Riley, before you go…" Don stood and scooted out from behind his computer, then approached Riley, who had paused before leaving the room. Hunter turned slightly to try to catch their exchange.

"You're studying to be a lawyer, right?"

"Yeah," she said brightly. "You in trouble with the law?" She laughed at her own joke, but Don shifted on his feet, no humor in his eyes.

"Nah, but I think I might need some help with something. You know anyone I could talk to?"

To Riley's credit, she got rid of her grin and stopped smacking her gum. "Depends. What's the problem?"

Don lowered his voice, but it still carried and Hunter heard every word.

"Genevieve's family is getting on my case. Accusing me of taking her money. I don't know what they're talking about. Say they're coming after me."

"Why would they accuse you of that?" Riley asked.

Don shook his head, his bushy white eyebrows drawn together. "Unexplained ATM withdrawals and extra cash back at the grocery store in the two weeks before her death. And two days after."

Hunter exchanged a glance with Triss. She was absorbing the conversation, too.

"Wow," Riley said, "But there would be video of the withdrawals. If you didn't do it, they won't pin it on you."

When Don didn't say anything, Riley's eyes widened. "*Did* you do it?"

He shook his head vehemently. "*No*—no, of course not."

"But?"

"But they say they have video of me."

"Have the police contacted you?" Riley asked.

"Well, no."

She nodded. "Okay, well, let me find someone for

you to talk to. It sounds like maybe this family is grasping at straws. If they had proof, you'd be arrested by now, don't you think? Sounds like they're harassing you."

"Her kids never did like me much," he agreed.

"Come with me, and I'll make a call," Riley said.

Hunter had a call to make, too. He needed to speak with Officer Goodson to see if they'd gotten any tips from the Hail family on misuse of her finances. On that note, he wondered if any of the other families of the deceased had noticed anything financially fishy.

Kaye appeared in the doorway just then. "Oh, good, the cameras are going up." She walked over to Triss and hugged her, ignoring the camera she was holding. "You look worlds better."

"I feel better," Triss replied.

"Still going on the lunch cruise with us?"

"Wouldn't miss it."

An uneasy feeling settled over Hunter as he tightened the final screw on the camera and stepped down from the ladder. He looked around the room, his gaze touching on the faces of the occupants. Nothing out of the ordinary. He was probably anxious about the lunch cruise.

Triss was walking toward the dining hall and he caught up with her. "Where you heading?"

She pointed to a far corner in the dining room. "This one goes there, right?"

He agreed.

"I'll get started on it." She started toward the corner, dragging a chair with her to stand on, but Hunter snagged her wrist.

"Hey."

She paused, her gaze flicking to his hand on her wrist and then up to his eyes.

"Any chance we can postpone the lunch cruise?" he asked, already knowing the answer.

She shook her head. "No way. There are no refunds, and everyone's been looking forward to it." She kept moving toward the far wall, tugging her arm away from his grasp. "I'm sure it'll be fine. It'd be a bold move to try something on the trip with such a small group of people."

That much was true. It would certainly limit the list of suspects. Hopefully, the attacker was smart enough to realize that and would stand down.

Cold and cloudy November days reminded Triss of the few hours she had held her daughter, and she wished she was anywhere but boarding the Inner Harbor lunch cruise, where she'd be expected to socialize for the next two hours.

Not for the first time, she wondered at how she had ever thought signing a contract with Harmony had been a good idea. Her mantra had been to fake it until she made it, and she had been surprised to discover that she didn't need to fake anything. She felt a genuine connection with many of the residents at Harmony, and she had tapped into a feeling that she had avoided for years—the warmth of friendship.

She had always loved too deeply. Had loved her mother for years, despite the lack of love returned. And she had fallen hard and fast for a high-school senior her freshman year, had been certain they'd get married. From the moment she had found out she was pregnant, she had loved her baby. Even before there was a heartbeat. Desperately, she had wished circumstances were different, that she could keep her.

She stood toward the end of the line as eighteen Harmony residents, her fellow grad students and several staff members began to board the enclosed ferry. She tugged her coat closer, her gaze drifting far out into the harbor as she remembered the warm press of newborn baby skin to her chest, the sharp black hair framing an impossibly tiny head, the perfect nose and pale pink lips. She had been gorgeous, perfect. And Triss had walked away.

"Can't believe they do these cruises in November," Hunter said next to her, and she shook away the memories.

"They don't usually. Brandon is always thinking up ideas and making them happen."

She glanced sideways at him, but he wasn't watching her. He was observing everyone ahead of them, his gaze scouting the area, touching on every face and every nook and cranny of the boat. She could almost see his mind working, evaluating risks, thinking through escape plans. She was glad he was here. With everything that had been happening at Harmony, the idea of bringing a group of seniors out into open water in November made her a little nervous. She just wished they had one or two more agents with them.

She finally reached the ramp and walked across it and into the enclosed bottom deck. Warmth seeped through her jacket, and she sighed with relief, looking around the large area. Dining tables were set elegantly around the perimeter of the enclosed deck, surrounded by nearly panoramic water views. Two buffet tables were set on either end, and classical music played softly.

"Here, let me see if I can do this," Kaye said as she stood in front of a fancy spread of desserts, flanked by Iris and Courtney. She was holding her phone in front of her as the three squeezed in an attempt at a selfie.

Triss unzipped her jacket but didn't take it off, still chilly from waiting in line outside. Residents and staff wandered the area, grinning and chatting, finding seats. The captain entered and welcomed them all, telling them important information about life vests and emergency procedures before discussing lunch and the sights they would sail by. Triss took a seat between Sissy and Iris, joining their conversation about a Christmas choral production they wanted to see together in a couple of weeks. Meanwhile, Hunter was taking a slow stroll around the room, pretending to take in the view from different windows, but she knew he was patrolling the area and keeping an eye out for any hidden dangers.

As the ship pulled away from the dock, though, Triss didn't feel nervous or sad anymore. She was caught up in conversation, the scent of garlic and onion filling the dining room as the luncheon was in full swing.

Of course, it didn't take long for the conversation around the room to turn to Triss's allergic reaction.

"You must be afraid to eat anything at this point," Kristy said from across the table. "I didn't realize dairy allergies could be so severe."

"It's scary," Triss conceded.

"You didn't know there was cheese in the ziti?" Riley asked, her expression perplexed.

"Barb made my meal with some substitutions for the cheese," Triss said. "Could be that I was allergic to one of the substitutions." She hoped that would shut down the topic because the luncheon didn't feel like the time to be discussing her suspicions. But Kaye looked at her seriously.

"Or it could be that your food got switched somehow."

Six pairs of eyes at the table stared at her as they all processed that idea.

"Oh, come on," Riley finally said, a tinny laugh erupting. "That's crazy talk."

But as Triss glanced around the table, she didn't see the humor or borderline hostility from earlier in the week. She saw mostly looks of concern and curiosity.

"I don't know," Sissy said, her mood unusually subdued. "Strange things have been happening. It's got me thinking. I mean, Genevieve was healthy as a horse. And Frank—suicide?"

"What are you saying, Sissy?" Iris asked.

Sissy shrugged. "Maybe just that we should all pay attention to our surroundings and let Triss and her hunky hero install all their cameras and alarms." The woman's eyes had glinted a little with her suggestion, and Triss had the feeling she was more interested in the theatrics of the idea of a killer in their midst than she was fearful of the possibility.

The others caught on and started laughing, but Triss didn't see the humor.

"I believe we'll be having a security meeting tomorrow," she said carefully. Now wasn't the time or place to dive into all her theories and concerns. No use scaring everyone on the lunch cruise when they wanted to relax and have a good time. "I will say that I think it's going to be very important, for a time, to be aware of your surroundings and go places in pairs."

The laughter died, and Kaye's expression sobered. "You don't have to tell me twice. Something just doesn't feel right."

Next to her, Courtney gathered her heavy sweater closer around her. Perpetually cold, she always dressed in multiple layers, but she looked more creeped out than cold at the moment.

"So, maybe we should revisit that security plan after all," Kaye said pleasantly.

As much as Triss was tempted to jump into this discussion, she knew she needed to wait until the meeting, when everyone was gathered together, and after she'd had a chance to firm up the plans with the others.

"We will, Kaye," she agreed. "For now, let's all try to enjoy ourselves."

"Sing us a song, Zach," Sissy called out. "That'll boost our spirits. And maybe it'll wake Iris up."

Triss looked over to see Iris's chin sag against her chest, her eyes closed.

Sissy nudged her. "Zach's about to sing for us. Wake up, Iris." She nudged her again.

Iris jerked awake, looking confused, and then smiled at Zach. "Oh, so he is. Can't stay awake today."

"You should go out on the deck," Zach said, pulling

out the guitar he brought everywhere. "The cold'll wake you up more than my singing." He tuned the guitar and began an acoustic serenade.

"You're looking sad, my dear," Kaye said to Courtney as she scooted her chair closer to their table. "Missing your grandfather?"

Courtney nodded, giving a half-hearted smile. "He's free, though," she said. "He was ready to go. He always told me he didn't want to live long enough to be in pain every day."

Kaye nodded. "Many a conversation around that topic happens at Harmony, that's for sure. How's your research project going?"

Courtney's eyes lit up. "It's coming along. You're one of the only people I haven't interviewed yet."

Kaye laughed. "Come on by my apartment whenever you want. I'm usually around, as you well know. Except for when I'm visiting my grandbabies."

Hunter moved around the dining room, chatting with different people at different tables, and Triss had begun to feel relaxed, even happy, until Kaye started talking about her daughters and grandchildren.

Triss's heart flipped as the conversation turned to baby showers and baby names, and she thought about how different life might have been. In less than two weeks, her own daughter would turn six, and Triss knew nothing about her. The thought rose swiftly and unexpectedly, like a punch in the gut. She excused herself to the bathroom, but on her way, the view beckoned. She walked out through a side door and found the stairs to the top deck. The cold air felt good on her face, and she took a deep breath, willing her thoughts to turn away from what couldn't be undone.

It was windier on the top deck, and she zipped her jacket, shoving her hands deep into her pockets and wrapping her soft knit scarf more snugly around her neck. The wind stung her eyes and she blinked away the tears, but didn't want to bring her hands out of her pockets to brush them away. The city beyond looked cold and sterile, the day dreary, and a heaviness settled at the base of her neck. She refused to dwell on it. She'd spent years learning how to move forward. Anyway, she was used to the depression that taunted her every November. She just needed to get through Thanksgiving and Christmas, and then she'd be fine again.

"There you are."

Hunter's voice startled her, and she turned to find him inches away. He smiled softly, but there was a question in his eyes. "It's warmer below. You look like you're about to turn into an ice cube." He frowned and stepped closer. "You're crying."

She laughed, the sound stolen by the wind. "No. It's the cold." Though, she couldn't be sure.

He blinked, his own eyes looking suddenly glossy. His eyebrows raised humorously. "Sure is."

He stood next to her and looked out at the harbor, silent for a time. "Do me a favor and let me know where you're going, okay? Scared me."

"Sorry." Another long silence fell over them, and she sensed that he was on the verge of asking all the questions he'd been suppressing since yesterday, when he'd found her daughter's things in her living-room chest. Or maybe all the questions he hadn't asked after she had deliberately stepped out of his life and away from his kids. She wasn't ready for any of those questions. "It's cold, anyway," she said, turning to go inside.

"Kind of refreshing."

"Two more minutes and you'll change your mind," she said. "I'm heading down."

But he said, "Wait," and she paused. The wind stung her eyes, her cheeks numb, but she turned back and looked him in the eye.

"I've got to ask—"

"Don't." Her pulse hammered in her ears, louder than the rush of the wind. She didn't even know what he was going to ask, but she knew she didn't want to answer it.

"Do I make you nervous?" he asked, anyway, and she frowned, confused.

Nervous, no. Terrified, yes. But she could never explain that to him, couldn't explain how much she wanted to give in to the pull of her heart, no matter the grief and pain it would bring for the sake of what just might be a happiness she had always assumed she couldn't have.

She raised an eyebrow. "Have you ever known me to be nervous?" she asked lightly, pretending not to take the question seriously.

"No." He stepped closer, his warmth encircling her, though inches still separated them. "Except for the past couple of days."

"Well, a lot's been going on to make me nervous."

"See, you're doing it again."

"What?"

"You stepped back." He stepped closer again.

She opened her mouth to argue, but involuntarily took another step back.

His eyes searched hers, and he took another small step.

This time, she didn't budge. The truth was, and she was horrified at the realization, that the closer he came, the more she fought the urge to close the gap. She hadn't been held in so long. Couldn't remember the last time she'd been held with tenderness and a sense of protection she could trust. And then Hunter had pulled her from her car, lifted her into his arms, carried her from the wreck. It had done something to her, that feeling of being held, cared for, protected, but she could fight it.

"What's going on, Triss?" he asked, but something had changed in his eyes, the brown dark and velvety, his intentions unmistakable.

"Nothing," she said, her voice a whisper. "I—"

But her words disappeared when his lips captured hers, all reasoning fleeing. His hands settled on her waist and drew her close, the warmth of his mouth on hers melting every barrier she'd built. She no longer felt the wind or the cold or the resistance of her heart—only the tug of an old, stomped-on dream that was desperate for revival.

The shrill pitch of a scream cut through the dreamlike haze, and Triss yanked away from Hunter, alarm sending ice down her spine. Not wasting a moment, she turned and ran for the steps, terrified of what she would see next.

SEVEN

"It's Iris!" Zach yelled as Triss and Hunter reached the bottom deck. He was frantically yanking at a bright red life preserver, Courtney catching up to him and attempting to help.

Dread formed a knot in Triss's gut, and she raced to the railing, peering over. The ferry was still moving, and she didn't see Iris.

She turned and caught Courtney's shocked gaze. "Tell the captain to cut the engine!" she yelled, and Courtney took off at a run.

"I see her!" Hunter pointed to a position closer to the boat than Triss had been looking, and she spotted Iris, too.

"Here!" Zach threw the life preserver over the side toward Iris, but it landed much too far away.

Below, the woman frantically treaded water, her face a pale dot in the cold black water, the boat leaving her quickly behind.

The boat's engine stopped, and the ferry started to turn to recover Iris. "She won't last much longer," Triss said. "The water's got to be freezing."

Hunter looked around and opened a bin full of life preservers. He grabbed out several and handed them to Triss. "Let's try to get one of these closer."

She grabbed the stack and jogged to the other side of the boat now that they were turning around. Hunter followed, along with what seemed like the rest of the passengers on the ship.

When Triss reached the other side, her hope tanked. "I don't see her." She scanned the black water and found the bright life preserver, but no pale face. Her stomach rolled. They were too late. *No.* She clutched the cold metal railing, desperately hoping she was wrong. That victim number five had not been claimed when she'd been up on the top deck kissing Hunter, of all things.

"There!" Hunter yelled, and she spotted Iris again. The woman was more still than before, her face nearly overcome by water. Still too far from the life preserver.

While Hunter tossed the first of his life preservers out at Iris, adrenaline consumed Triss, and common sense failed her. She yanked off her coat, snapped on a life preserver, kicked off her shoes and jumped

"Triss, no!" Hunter yelled as he realized what she was doing, his hand grazing her shoulder too late as she plunged into the icy water below.

The shock of it stunned her, disoriented her for a moment. She shouldn't have jumped in. The water was so cold, so choppy. This was now bound to be a rescue mission for two because of her reckless move. She gasped in a harsh breath of frigid air and focused on location. The boat was to her back, the life preserver to her left. She turned right, searching for Iris but not seeing her. She had to be close. She'd jumped in nearly on top of the woman.

She heard shouting from above and angled her head up, saw Hunter pointing directly to her right.

"She went under!" he yelled as he threw on a life jacket, clearly ready to jump in after her.

"Wait!" Triss shouted, finding her voice. She'd started this. She'd see it through. And they'd need Hunter to help them back into the boat.

She forgot the cold, ignored the numbness seeping into her limbs. She had to start moving. Clumsily, she pushed forward, the life preserver more of a hindrance than a help. Blindly, she waved her arms through the dark waters, hoping against all hope that she would come in contact with Iris.

Please, let me find her. Let her be okay. It was a prayer she had no faith would be heard, let alone answered, but it was all she had as she fought the hopelessness.

Then, her right leg slid against something, and she turned, frantic, knowing it was Iris. Iris, under the water. Iris, sinking! She ducked her head under the water and forced her eyes open, searching the shadows. There! She could see her, but she was sinking too fast!

Triss's fingers were barely working, numbness setting in, but she pinched at the fasteners of her life preserver, anyway, managing to unlatch herself. She let the preserver float away, took a deep breath and plunged deep toward Iris.

She could see her, could almost reach her. She kicked her feet with the last of her energy, gathered enough strength to reach the drowning woman and caught hold of her arm.

Triss was almost out of air, and she knew it. Still, she wrapped an arm around the woman's slight body and started reaching toward the surface.

She pulled at the water with her free hand, kicked with her legs, but she wasn't getting far enough fast enough. Her lungs burned as if they would burst, and Triss suddenly realized she wasn't going to make it. She'd have to let go of Iris, get another breath and come back for her. She hoped it wouldn't be too late.

But just as she started to slide her arm away from the woman, a heavy swirl of water enveloped her, a firm hand grabbing her wrist. Hunter! She tightened her grip on Iris and willed her lungs to hold out until she finally broke the surface.

Hunter shoved a life preserver at her, and she grabbed it with one hand as he pulled Iris from her arms and dragged her limp body toward the boat. Triss's entire body felt numb, her limbs moving in slow motion as she swam closer to the boat. But her heart ached, grief welling up strong and deep as she watched Iris's body being pulled out of the frigid waters, and she knew that she'd been too late.

The ferry was relatively small, the distance from the deck to the water no more than fifteen feet, but getting into the boat with Triss and Iris took far too long. By the time they'd reached the deck, Hunter wasn't hopeful Iris would survive.

The captain appeared as Hunter set Iris on the deck,

rolling her to her side. A small amount of water emptied from her mouth, and he turned her head.

"CPR," the captain said grimly, kneeling by Iris's head and taking over immediately. As the captain gave rescue breaths, Hunter realized the boat was heading back to shore. He turned to Triss, who was already wrapped in blankets, the crew tending to her to warm her up as Kaye came toward her with a steaming mug of what was probably tea. Triss hated tea, but he had a feeling she wouldn't refuse it.

He'd thought he'd lost her. Her reckless jump from the ferry had taken him by surprise, but he'd known that three in the water would just complicate the situation. So he'd waited, against his intuition, when she went under to search for Iris. Then he'd seen her life preserver and expected her to pop up at any second. He'd told himself to count to forty-five seconds before he jumped in, but he'd only gotten to thirty. Instinct had told him Triss was in trouble.

Kaye held the mug up to Triss's blue-tinged lips, and Triss drank, her eyes wide with shock as a crew member tucked a blanket closer around her wet hair and neck.

The cold suddenly hit Hunter then, a tremor taking hold. He ignored it, turning to the captain. "Tell me how to help."

"Take over chest compressions."

Together, they worked for long minutes, but Iris was showing no signs of life as the shore drew closer. And then, suddenly, as the captain bent to give another set of rescue breaths, Iris coughed.

Hunter helped turn her over as she expelled what seemed like a bathtub full of water.

Shock and relief settled over the captain's sun-weathered face.

"We need some blankets over here!" Hunter called out, but the crew was two steps ahead and already rounding the corner with armloads of blankets. One was dropped onto his shoulders, and people began piling the others around Iris.

As the warmth of the blanket started to cut the chill, Hunter's senses began to clear and he searched the faces that had crowded onto the deck.

The residents huddled together in groups, many patting one another's backs or wiping tears from their faces. Zach and Courtney stood off to one side, Zach's arm protectively on her shoulders. Kristy was helping a couple of crew members tend to Triss, and the Harmony staff all seemed to be milling around vigilantly as they began to encourage everyone to seek the warmth inside.

What had happened? How had Iris gone overboard? Hunter turned to the rail, considered how he'd had to hoist himself up onto it before he jumped. Was there a broken railing? He stood, his wet clothes as heavy and cold as blocks of ice. The blanket wasn't doing much good, but he forced himself to walk the perimeter of the deck, checking the railing as he walked. It took mere minutes to scout the area, and he didn't find any clues as to how Iris, a woman who couldn't be much more than five feet and a hundred pounds, had simply fallen overboard.

There was no doubt in his mind someone had meant

for her to be victim number five. He hurried to the dining area, where everyone had taken shelter from the elements. If someone had pushed Iris, that same person might be willing to do anything to make sure she couldn't live to tell the story.

He opened the door and entered the large room, the welcome heat bringing a measure of relief, despite the sharp pains as his fingers and toes began to warm up. Whereas earlier the room had been filled with a peaceful air of conversation and quiet music, now it was stretched with tension, nervous energy vibrating off every occupant.

He spotted Triss sitting on the edge of a bench, where Iris had been settled atop a makeshift cushion of several stacked blankets. More blankets lifted Iris's head, and though she looked as white as frost, her eyes were alert as several of her friends hovered over her.

Hunter made his way to the group, noting Kaye, Sissy, George and Mack. Triss's fellow grad students had congregated nearby and were casting worried glances toward Iris.

Triss looked up as he approached. Her dark hair sat in heavy, wet waves, and she pulled the navy blanket tighter around her still-shivering shoulders. The blanket was soaked through.

"Let me round up another blanket for you," he said. "We need to get you warmer."

"Here."

He turned to find Brandon approaching, already holding out two blankets. "One for you both."

"Thanks." Hunter accepted the blankets and turned to Triss, who was already shedding her soaked one.

He set the blanket on her shoulders and drew it closed as she sat again, her eyes dropping from his. The memory of the kiss they'd shared flashed through his mind. It had been unplanned, unexpected and probably the wrong move. But it hadn't felt like the wrong move at the time. And he knew now, with more certainty than he'd ever had, that he was not going to be able to simply walk away from Triss.

"She doesn't know what happened," Triss said quietly, her gaze on Iris, who was listening intently to Kaye's words of encouragement.

"Nothing?"

"She went outside because she kept falling asleep. She thought the cold air would wake her up."

"And then?"

Triss shook her head. "Nothing." Then she looked up at Hunter, her brown eyes the darkest of espresso. "But we do have something."

He nodded, glancing around the room. "A list." They had a finite list of suspects here, and this was something they could give to Officer Goodson. He'd spoken to the officer on the phone on the way over to the harbor, and the news had been unsettling. Yes, the Hail family had reported suspected misuse of Genevieve's finances, and yes, they were investigating and speaking with the other families. The officer couldn't divulge any more details. The fire inspector hadn't been much help, either, stating that they had no more clues from the fire. The smoke detectors had been tampered with, which led them to suspect arson, but they wouldn't know more until accelerant test results came in—which could take another couple of weeks.

The boat pulled up to the dock then, emergency vehicle lights flashing through the cloudy day and into the wide-windowed cabin. Hunter gripped the cold railing with frustration. Hopefully, Vince and Adam were well on their way to installing the new security equipment, and maybe Harrison would have something for them by the time they returned. He knew that running their own investigations was risky and could interfere with an eventual court case, but if they waited on proper protocols and police, someone else was going to wind up dead.

"What do you have for us?" Hunter asked as Triss led Harrison into her small living room. The new place was furnished, but bare, and Hunter suspected Triss would leave it that way.

Harrison sat on one of the living-room chairs and pulled his laptop from his briefcase. "A few things," he said as he opened the laptop, his expression serious.

Triss took the seat next to him, her hair almost dry, thick waves making her look even younger than her twenty-two years. He'd only ever seen her hair pin-straight, but the waves made her seem softer somehow. Which was probably why she made a point of straightening it, he reasoned.

She caught him looking and quickly looked away. They'd been at Harmony for nearly two hours, but they hadn't had much time to speak. Officer Goodson had arrived with his partner again, and had been interviewing each person who had been on the boat. They'd circle back and interview the ferry crew as well. Meanwhile, Hunter had been helping Vince and Adam install security cameras and set up the monitoring software on the new computers. They'd need more time to get all the locks changed out, even with help from Shield.

Triss looked impatient as Harrison's fingers flew across his keyboard. Hunter suspected he knew why. She needed to be at work in a couple of hours, and the security team had yet to announce the new security plan to the residents and staff. Vince and Adam had assured her they'd take care of it before dinner, but that wasn't looking likely.

"The good news is that Don is in the clear, so far," Harrison finally said. He turned the monitor toward them—a dating web site was on the screen, Don's profile featured with a photo that looked a decade old and the caption "Seeking Soulmate."

"So, that's why he keeps getting on a computer in the corner," Triss said, amusement playing over her face.

"Isn't it a little soon to be looking for a date?" Hunter asked. "Genevieve died, what, two weeks ago?"

Triss's smile fell and she nodded. "True."

"People get lonely," Harrison remarked. "Of course, we can't exclude him completely, but his digital fingerprint is clean as far as I can see."

"And he wasn't on the ferry today," Triss pointed out.

"Okay, what else did you find?" Hunter asked.

Harrison pulled up another screen, and Hunter leaned closer for a better look.

"Instructions on how to create a timed detonator," Harrison explained. "And ways one might conceal it."

Hunter's pulse picked up as he met Harrison's serious eyes. "Like under the gas cap of a vehicle." Someone had planted a device on Triss's car. This was information that needed to be handed over to the police.

"Who?" Triss asked, her body statue-still.

"Unfortunately, we don't know. Whoever ran this search knew Frank Townsend's log-in information. The search was run two days after his death, under his account, well after midnight."

"Who has access to computer passwords and log-ins?" Hunter asked.

"We have an IT guy who works here a few hours a week," Triss said. "Other than that, it's anyone's guess. I mean, I've helped a bunch of residents with getting logged in and setting up email and social-media accounts. I'm sure others have, too."

Others who might make a habit of jotting down user-names and passwords for nefarious use.

"Do you remember anyone helping Frank with the computer?" Hunter asked.

Triss shook her head. "Honestly? Most of us probably did. He'd never touched a computer until he moved into Harmony."

"Who's 'most of us'?" Harrison asked as he closed his laptop and put it away.

"The other grad students, the staff. I wouldn't be surprised if Frank called Barb out of the kitchen to help."

Harrison stood. "I'll come by over the weekend and keep working. Anything else you need from me?"

"I'll let you know," Hunter responded, following him to the door. "Appreciate the help."

Harrison said goodbye and stepped out, and Hunter knew he should, too. Instead, he shut the door behind the young technology whiz and turned to the bare living room.

Triss eyed him warily from her chair. It was hard to believe that she was the same woman who, just hours ago, had leaned blissfully into a kiss unlike any he'd ever experienced. That kiss had stripped away what Hunter had long suspected was a facade of cold indifference, and there was no going back now.

All the reasons he had for not pursuing a relationship with Triss—the fact that she was six years younger than him, the fear that he would hold her back from her career ambitions, his uncertainty about her feelings for him and his kids—didn't matter anymore. He was logical enough to know that love could conquer all of those misgivings. Not that he would call this love just yet, but he didn't have another word for it—the magnetic draw that he felt toward her, the compelling desire to understand her, the way his heart tripped when she walked into a room, or when she wrapped her arms around one of his kids.

"I've got to get ready for work," she said pointedly, no indication in her expression that she even remembered the kiss they had shared.

It was his cue to leave, but he'd spent too long letting her get away with avoidance.

"I won't stay long," he said, walking to the living room and sitting in the chair directly across from her.

She was sitting curled up in the oversize chair, her palms resting on her knees, her relaxed posture at odds with the sudden alertness in her eyes.

He suspected he only had seconds before she bolted, and he leaned forward, sliding a hand over one of hers and wrapping his fingers under the warmth of her palm.

"We made a good team today," he said.

She slid her hand out from under his. "Good training does that," she said simply, her cordial attitude in full force.

"So we're back where we started," Hunter said quietly, more confused than upset.

She sent him a quizzical look.

"Pretending there's nothing going on between us," he clarified, unable to curb his own directness. He'd told himself he wouldn't push for a relationship that didn't seem like it was going to work. Had reminded himself that all his pushing years ago had ended up in Viv's death. What was it about Triss that made him want to keep pushing?

For a moment, her gaze softened, but he read only sadness there. "Obviously, there's something here, Hunter," she said finally. "But it won't work."

"What am I missing?" he asked, carefully keeping his tone relaxed despite his hammering pulse and the real temptation to kiss her again—if for nothing else than to prove that this kind of connection wasn't one people just walked away from for no clear reason.

Her gaze flicked away from him for a split second, as if she was trying to come up with a believable story. He'd never known Triss to lie, and he hoped she wouldn't start now.

"For one, our lives are too different," she began, looking suddenly quite matter-of-fact.

"Different, yes, but not an impossible obstacle," he pointed out reasonably. "Triss, today, when we—"

"You caught me off guard with the kiss, Hunter," she said, cutting him off, as if she knew exactly what he was going to say. And maybe she did. She seemed to know him and understand him in a way that even his late wife hadn't been able to. "Chemistry does not solve all the problems."

She was staring so seriously at him that he had to work hard at not grinning. "Usually, that's true," he said, his attention drawn to the curve of her lips. "But this kind of chemistry…"

She stood abruptly, and he looked up at her questioningly.

"Even this kind of chemistry doesn't solve everything," she said.

"What's the other problem, then?" Hunter asked. "Maybe there's another way to solve it. Unless there's a secret husband somewhere. That would be a tough one," he joked softly, in an attempt to ease the tension in her expression.

She looked at him for a moment so long that he found himself wondering if, perhaps, she did have a secret husband. The idea was ludicrous, but it was obvious that Triss was hiding something.

"No husbands, secret or otherwise," she said finally,

but she didn't smile. "My other reasons are private, Hunter. I need to ask you to respect that."

He wanted to respect it, but his heart told him otherwise. Sensing she was about to kick him out, anyway, he stood to leave. Instead of walking toward the door, though, he paused, mere inches of charged air separating them. "I can do that," he managed to say. He'd have to figure out how, but he'd do what she asked. Still, he read sadness in her eyes and a longing that didn't match the words she'd spoken to him.

"Thank you," she whispered finally, but instead of reaching for the door to usher him out, she stepped closer and slid her arms around his waist, the warmth of her embrace enveloping him. She rested her cheek against his chest, her thick black waves grazing Hunter's jaw. The hug caught him by surprise, but he didn't miss a beat. He pressed a kiss to the top of her head and smoothed his hands up and down her back for a long moment. She was a contradiction he didn't know what to do with. In the same breath that she told him they could never work out, she was reaching for him. It was true that chemistry could not overcome all obstacles, but this was more than chemistry—this deep connection of souls, this knowing one another so intimately that unanswered questions didn't seem to matter.

"I'll respect your privacy and not ask you to tell me your other reasons," he said against her hair. "But I'm still going to try to prove you're wrong."

EIGHT

Triss sighed, closing her eyes against the comforting slide of Hunter's palms along her back, the warmth of his breath near her ear. This hug was definitely not conducive to keeping her distance. Dredging up enough willpower to move, she pulled away. Hunter immediately let his hands drop to his sides, giving her space. She crossed her arms over her chest as if that might keep her from stepping into his arms again. Her eyelashes were suspiciously damp, though she didn't think she'd been crying. But there was something so right and easy about being with Hunter. Sometimes, she felt like maybe nothing did matter. Maybe she could move on from her past and pick up with a new start in life.

Hunter's deep brown eyes searched hers, that perpetual light in his gaze tugging at her heart. His kids shared that trademark sense of humor and lightheartedness. She did not, though she craved it. Guilt panged at the thought. It was torture, knowing Hunter, and his Levi and Josie. It was as if God Himself had put them in her life to say "See, this is the kind of life you could have had." Only, she had bailed. And even though a small part of her heart wondered if Hunter and his kids were her chance at redemption, she knew the reality. If she said yes to them, she was also saying yes to daily grieving, as she experienced all she had turned her back on when she'd kissed her daughter goodbye six years ago.

"This is too much all at once," she finally said to Hunter, who seemed to be practicing his fail-safe interrogation strategy of long silences. "Let's concentrate on figuring out what's going on around here for now?"

He was silent for a moment, but then agreed. "Fair enough. For now."

"I've got to shower, so I'm kicking you out," Triss said, even though she had the strangest desire to call in sick. She was constantly working, achieving, planning. It kept her from thinking and regretting. Only now, for the first time in years, she felt like she could use some downtime to think. She'd been ready to tell Hunter to get a replacement for his shift at Harmony, and then she'd stepped right into his arms. Her own actions were confusing to her.

Hunter made his way to her door, turning to her once more before he left. "I'll be outside if you need me."

She locked the door behind him and went straight to her room. Except for the provided bed and dresser, it was bare. Smoke damage had ruined many of her clothes, and she hadn't had a chance to shop. Thankfully, sweet Kaye had washed some of the salvageable clothes for her. She grabbed a pair of dress slacks, a blazer and a white oxford, then hurried to the bathroom to shower.

She emerged from her apartment nearly an hour later, having rejected all dwelling on Hunter and pushing herself directly into work mode. With barely enough time to dry her hair and not enough time to flat-iron it, she scraped it into a tidy topknot and yanked on her blazer. She didn't have much time to eat something before heading out for her shift.

Hunter pushed away from the wall as she walked out, his dimpled smile making her heart leap.

"Just in time," he said. "Vince and Adam are starting the meeting in the commons."

Dinner would have to wait.

All of Creekside Manor had gathered for the meeting, and extra chairs had been brought in from the dining hall. Residents, grad students and staff were all present. Vince and Adam would have to repeat the presentation at Silverwood and Emerald—there simply wasn't a room large enough to accommodate everyone at once. Also, Triss would venture to guess that some of the rules would be different at the other home sites.

"Looks like everyone's here," Vince said, shoving his too-long comb-over out of his eyes. "This won't take long—just want to keep you all informed." He pointed to a camera in one corner of the room. "We're installing some extra cameras throughout the property, as you can see," he said. "Should be all set in a couple of days. Then we'll work on installing new locks and—"

"Hold on there. How many cameras are you installing?" George Wyrick asked. "And where are they?"

Vince shrugged as if the question was pointless. "Around ten, mostly outside."

Hunter stood then. "Mind if I chime in here, Vince?"

Vince nodded.

Hunter walked up to the front. "Good to see you all here this evening. I've met most of you by now. I'm Hunter Knox, one of Triss's friends." He motioned to Triss to join him, so she followed his lead. "We're working with Shield Protection Services to help make sure that all the security protocols and equipment here are up-to-date. We're installing a total of twelve additional cameras on the property, and we're upgrading the four current cameras. Eight of those cameras are installed around the property outside, mostly at points of entry. The additional cameras are installed in common areas inside the facilities here."

"Just as long as you're not putting hidden cameras in bathrooms!" Riley called out with amusement. "I was just watching the news about some creep who owned a hotel doing that, and—"

"Wait, what? I don't want any cameras in my bathroom!" Sissy called out.

"Calm down, Sissy," Kaye said, patting her arm. "No one wants to be a fly on the wall in any of our bathrooms."

Triss suppressed a laugh as Hunter more or less took over the presentation, which was for the best, considering Vince seemed reluctant and a bit put out to have to deal with new systems and protocols, and Adam seemed distracted, constantly checking his cell phone and looking at the clock, his uniform shirt hanging loose on his gaunt frame. Triss zeroed in on him, noting dark circles under his eyes, and hair that had grown a bit too long, curling at the nape and around his ears. She hadn't seen much of Adam lately, but she'd need to check in with him because he was looking rough.

Hunter continued to inform everyone about the two other major changes: the installation of new locks and distribution of key cards throughout the next week, as well as new security protocols for visitors.

"Do we get a say in any of this?" Don asked suddenly, and all eyes turned to him. Sprawled out, with one arm casually draped over the chair Hunter had previously occupied, he did not appear on first glance to be upset.

"We're always open to suggestions and feedback," Hunter said diplomatically.

"Well, I can get on board with the cameras and the locks and the key cards. But the visitor logs are overboard. I mean, Mack pops into my apartment every hour most days and—"

"Every hour?" Mack asked, indignant.

"Maybe not every hour, but—"

"I won't pop by at all tomorrow then, if that's the way you feel, and—"

"I'm not saying—"

"Okay, gentlemen," Hunter interrupted. "This conversation can happen later, but I hear what you're saying. You're used to your friends visiting, and you visiting your friends."

"Last thing we all want to do is sign in and sign out whenever we go to each other's places," George asserted.

"Housekeepers are one thing," Kaye said. "And even, no offense to the newcomers—you are all lovely—but even the grad students or new employees that we don't know well yet. But I tend to agree that having friends sign in is overkill."

Triss watched Hunter as he listened to concerns rise up, and she wondered how he would respond. She needed to get going soon.

"That's a valid concern," Hunter said. "What we'd like to do is run a two-week trial period with the new system and protocols. Then we can invite feedback and make adjustments if we need to. How does that sound?"

What they didn't know was that Shield hoped to have caught the culprit by then.

"I can live with that," Don said.

Triss started to excuse herself, but Hunter signaled for her to wait.

"I'll be around tomorrow if anyone needs to talk with me. My partner, Bryan, just arrived, and I'm heading out. Vince, want to take any other questions?"

Vince stood, and Hunter caught up with Triss as Bryan walked through the door.

Bryan handed Triss a key fob. "Got a car outside for you. Roman's lending you one of the old BMWs."

"Thanks," Triss said, unable to hide her surprise. She'd assumed she'd be reliant on Hunter or Bryan to drive her everywhere for the next week or so until she could purchase a new vehicle.

"He said you can use it through the end of the year. Buys you some time."

Triss made a mental note to thank Roman and said goodbye to Bryan, who would be patrolling the property and working on installing new locks throughout the night shift.

Hunter walked next to her as they stepped out into the cold evening air. "You look exhausted," he said, his gaze observant, and her mind flashed to the brush of his lips on hers, the safe warmth of his embrace.

"I'll be fine," she answered.

"Maybe tonight, but the zoo will be a challenge tomorrow," he said, tired amusement in his voice. "Five kindergartners and Levi. There's not enough sleep or caffeine to power through this one."

The zoo. Josie's birthday. Triss had completely forgotten. She needed to bail. It was too much. He would understand, could see how tired she was. But she'd get some sleep and see how she felt around noon before she decided.

"Speaking of which, Roman said he'll get you to Harmony in the morning. He'll stick around until my relief can get here around nine to cover my shift. I'll text you when we're on our way to pick you up for Josie's party."

Triss nodded, still contemplating how she might back out. "Sounds good."

"I'll follow you to the job location and then head home."

Triss considered telling him to go on home now. No way was anyone able to tamper with the Shield BMW. She'd be safe enough tonight. But she knew it would be a futile argument, so she thanked him and turned to the car, using the key fob to unlock it.

Hunter reached toward her, but she sidestepped him quickly.

He paused, his gaze assessing. Then he continued to reach around the door to grab the handle and pull it open for her. Triss's cheeks warmed as she realized he hadn't been reaching for her at all.

Hunter held the door open, stepping behind it as if sensing her inner turmoil. She climbed in and yanked on her seat belt, feeling foolish.

"Drive safe," he said. "I'll be right behind you." He pressed the door shut.

It was going to be a long night. She hadn't even had a few hours to sleep this afternoon, and she hadn't eaten. Still, despite her tough schedule, she was disciplined enough to make it work. She went to school Mondays through Thursdays, then worked the night shift at Shield Fridays through Sundays. She made it work by getting plenty of sleep during weeknights and managing a few hours of sleep on weekend afternoons. This week had thrown off her schedule. She blinked away the heaviness behind her eyes as the sun disappeared. No one would have blamed her if she'd called off, but it wasn't in her makeup. Unless she was on death's door, Triss didn't take a sick day.

She'd make up for the lack of sleep tomorrow, she told herself as the client's residence came into view. Brittany Wellington had a Keurig and always left out plenty of coffee for guests and employees. Triss would need more than a cup or two to get her through the night.

If nothing else, it was a quiet shift, and she'd have

plenty of time to think. There had to be something they were missing. She parked her car at the Wellington estate and got out, waving goodbye to Hunter as she hurried up to the front entrance. She kept thinking about Iris going overboard. It seemed unlikely she had fallen over a railing that nearly came to her chest. But if someone had thrown her overboard, what would the motive be?

Don's conversation with Riley came back to her then, and she hit upon an angle they needed to pursue. As she entered the foyer of the large home and waved to her partner, she called Hunter.

"Everything okay?" he asked.

"I had a thought," she answered. "We need to have Iris check her bank statements for any suspicious activity. And ask if she's had any help with setting up accounts or anything like that."

"Good idea," Hunter said. "If we can find a motive, we might find the culprit."

"Hopefully we'll find both soon," Triss said, but as she hung up with Hunter, she couldn't shake a dark sense of foreboding.

She pocketed her phone and forced herself into work mode, logging into the tablet to check off the areas as she patrolled throughout the night. She turned toward the kitchen of the eight-thousand-square-foot home. But first, coffee.

When her alarm woke her up at 11:00 a.m., Triss was still exhausted. Granted, after getting home from work at half past six, she'd only managed to get about four hours of sleep, but that wasn't typically a problem for her. The room was dark, the day overcast with cold rain. She yanked open the blackout curtains, but the dreariness outside didn't do much to imbue her with energy. Maybe the zoo birthday would be canceled. It certainly wasn't a good day for it. She checked the forecast and saw that it was going to clear up soon. No messages from Hunter, so the party must still be on.

She sat on the end of her bed, phone in hand. It was time to be rational. She was one year away from finishing grad school, with a spring internship lined up with the FBI forensics department at the Baltimore headquarters. She'd spent years working toward her career goals, and she knew that her first job out of graduate school would probably mean relocating to another city, at least. Likely, another state.

There was no room in her plan for a family. She had not even written a family into her goals. She'd known herself well enough at the age of sixteen to realize that she could never handle love and loss again.

She'd been terrified to discover she was pregnant. Scared and ashamed. She couldn't bring herself to tell Luke, who had given up everything to raise her and their brother, Cal. When her boyfriend had given her the money for the abortion and driven her to the clinic, she hadn't known what else to do.

He'd waited in the truck, smoking his cigarette, the windows closed against the harshly cold early winter day. She'd gone inside the sterile little clinic alone, the cash stuffed deep in the pockets of jeans she could barely button over her growing stomach.

She'd signed in and sat in the waiting room, and her hands had involuntarily settled on the barely notice-able curve of her belly. She was nearly sixteen weeks. She'd put off the appointment for as long as she could, but knew she wouldn't be able to hide the truth much longer. She'd told only her boyfriend, and she had never felt more alone. What she hadn't told him was that late at night, she'd been waking up to this strange fluttery feeling in her stomach. She knew it was early still, and she'd tried to convince herself the feeling could not pos-sibly be the baby moving.

But as she sat in the room waiting to be called to terminate her pregnancy, she felt it again, stronger this time, the flutter vibrating against the palms of her hands. She wasn't ignorant. She'd looked up the stages of a fetus, knew that her baby had every baby part and a heartbeat. The only thing keeping this little one from survival would be her.

Someone called her name, and she stood, woodenly, following the nurse into the hallway, but as she walked, the fluttering continued, and her heartache grew.

"Can I use the restroom?" she'd asked suddenly, and the nurse paused, her gaze observant. She pointed to a nearby hallway.

"On the left."

Triss walked down the hall, but she didn't look for the bathroom. Her eyes were trained on the exit sign at the end of the hallway.

She picked up her pace.

"You just missed it, hon," the nurse called out.

Triss ran.

She burst through the back door and into soft snow flurries in the tiny parking lot. It was empty, save for a giant dumpster. She wondered what might be in that dumpster. For a split second, she thought about running to the front of the building to tell her soon-to-be ex, Pete, that she couldn't do it. She'd ask him to take her home, and then confess to Luke.

Instead, she'd kept running. She wasn't far from the train station, after all, and she had a decent wad of money.

Several months later, she'd returned home. Luke had accepted her back, few questions asked. And she made a vow to herself never to love that deeply again. The kind of love she had felt for her tiny baby was unlike anything she'd ever experienced. And handing her over to her adoptive parents had nearly undone her.

The only thing that had kept Triss from taking her own life in the weeks after was the knowledge that Luke would eventually find out. And he would be devastated. She couldn't do that to him.

She stared at her phone, an image of Josie and Levi coming to mind, particularly the day they'd shared at their home making a royal mess out of a cake-baking attempt. She'd offered to help him because he'd been in a bind. She couldn't have known how much she would love his kids. Then she thought about the uncertain but hopeful look in Josie's eyes when she'd walked into Harmony the other day and seen Triss for the first time in months.

She couldn't do it. She couldn't open the door to that kind of love. If she did, she would be all in. And she'd have to tell Hunter about her daughter. And, if she told Hunter, she'd have to tell Luke. The two worked together a lot, and if Hunter ever slipped and Luke heard it from him… Triss sighed. She didn't want her brother to know. He would be crushed. He would ask why she hadn't told him. Worse, he would tell her what she knew now with six years of growing up behind her: he would have helped her raise her little girl.

She didn't want to hear that, even though she knew it was true. She didn't want to think about the mistake she had made, or wonder if her daughter was well loved. She didn't want to own up to a six-year secret that was tied up in a whole bundle of lies. And the truth was? She didn't deserve the chance to be a mom. She'd had it once, and she'd turned her back.

Her eyes swam with tears, her throat clogging up. Even if she decided to come clean and tell Hunter and Luke, and then tried to give a relationship with Hunter a chance…she couldn't live with the daily reminders of what she'd missed out on. The zoo birthday was one event on a never-ending list of reminders she'd face if she said yes to Hunter Knox. And he and his kids didn't deserve to contend with her haywire emotions on their special days and during their important milestones.

Resolutely, she started punching out a text to Hunter—she would bow out of the birthday party. It was better for everyone, herself included, if she maintained her distance.

She sent the text and forced herself to get up, tucking the covers quickly over her bed and heading to her closet. She was itching to go on a run, convinced that missing so many workouts this week was contributing to her mood. It was nearly lunch, though, and she wanted to go have a chat with Iris. She'd start running again the next morning.

"Stay in your room, Josie!" Hunter called, shoving open the door with his hip as he brought the large ladybug-shaped sheet cake into the house, several bags looped on his arms.

"I'm guarding the door," Samantha said from the hall, her voice cheerful, as per usual. "Levi's in there, too."

"Good call," Hunter said, reminded once again of how fortunate he was to have found Samantha. He didn't know what he'd do when she inevitably left her nanny job for a teaching position next fall. She'd become almost like an older sister to the kids, and they had created a comfortable foursome in the house.

He set down the cake on the counter and the bags on the floor. He didn't have much time to wrap the gifts or make the goody bags. Thankfully, Samantha could keep the kids busy while he took care of those jobs. He found a shelf in the fridge for the cake, and then transported the gifts to his bedroom. Shutting the door behind him, he locked it and let Samantha know the kids could be freed.

He made quick work of all the goody bags, then set his attention to gift-wrapping. As he stacked the final box on top of the other wrapped gifts, he found himself fighting that too-familiar feeling of emptiness.

He looked at the stack of gifts on the floor, the basket of goody bags nearby, the pile of balloons hanging on the doorknob. Funny how the moments he should be happiest ended up being the moments he felt the most alone. It was during the birthdays, the first days of school, the tooth-fairy nights and the Christmas cookie baking when he felt the heaviness of single parenthood, and the deep loss of not having someone to share the special moments with.

He checked his watch. Almost time to get going. He grabbed his phone to let Triss know they would be heading her way in a few minutes, but she'd already texted him. He frowned when he read her message, but he didn't have a right to be disappointed. Triss was exhausted. She'd had a rough week, and she'd be back on the night shift at Shield tonight. He couldn't expect her to spend a couple of hours out in the cold at the zoo with a bunch of six-year-olds, especially when she had been trying to make it clear that whatever was between them couldn't work. He suspected that minor detail had more to do with her canceling than her physical exhaustion. Triss had more energy and drive than anyone he'd ever met.

Hopefully, Josie wouldn't be too upset. She was probably so excited about her birthday and her friends that she wouldn't miss Triss. After all, they'd barely seen each other since August.

He pulled two balloons out of the bunch—a purple sparkly one and a blue one with a light inside—then opened his door.

"Who's ready for a birthday party?" he called.

The kids came running, squealing. He looped the

balloons on their wrists and told them to help bring the presents to the kitchen. They'd meet their friends at the zoo and then come to the house for presents and cake later.

"What's in dis one, Dad? What's in dis one?" Levi asked, hanging on to the wrapped Easy-Bake Oven that Hunter knew he would regret purchasing.

"I know what these are!" Josie announced, holding a stack of three books he'd wrapped without a box to disguise them. She was an insatiable reader, and he couldn't keep up. Normally, he checked out stacks at the library for her, but for the past couple of birthdays and Christmases, he'd bought her a set of three new books and she'd been thrilled to receive them, often reading her favorites again and again when she'd gone through her library stacks.

"Time to go!" Hunter said, and Samantha gave the kids hugs.

"Sorry I can't come," she told Josie, "but I left you a special gift."

"That's okay, Samantha. Thank you."

Samantha was a live-in nanny, but Hunter tried to give her the weekends off when he could. As much as she loved Josie, she also had a boyfriend she didn't get to spend a lot of time with, and Hunter figured that a date night was more appealing to the college-aged girl than an afternoon with her charges and a bunch of giggly friends.

Minutes later, he was securing Levi into his car seat as Josie began buckling herself in. He knew she wouldn't forget about Triss, so he decided he may as well tell her now.

"We're going to head straight to the zoo to meet your friends instead of picking up Triss, Josie. She couldn't make it after all, but said she—"

"What?" Josie stilled, her seat belt not yet clicked into place. "She said she was coming."

"I know, but sometimes people's plans change," Hunter said, realizing worriedly that Josie's cheeks were ruddy, her nose suddenly pink. "She wanted to come, but—"

"And I wanted her to come," Josie said in a small voice, and the tears started.

Hunter finished strapping Levi into his seat and then walked around to the other side of the truck, fighting sadness for his daughter and a surprising trickle of anger toward Triss. That wasn't fair. How was she to know how upset Josie would be?

He crouched next to her and kissed her forehead and cheek, wiping her tears with his palm. "I'm sorry, sweetie," he said gently. "I hate to see you sad on your birthday. But all your friends are going to be there, and there are so many animals we're going to see. Also, I planned a little surprise. Want me to tell you about it?"

She sniffled and nodded.

"You and your friends are going to get to help give a baby elephant a bath!"

Josie laughed through her tears. "Really?"

He smiled, relieved that she was reaching for happiness again. "Now, are you ready to get this show on the road?"

She nodded emphatically and wiped away her tears. Hunter kissed her cheek, then double-checked her seat belt before he shut her door and walked around to the driver's seat.

But as he pulled away from the house, his attention caught on the rearview mirror, which revealed an expression on Josie's face that yanked at his heart. He'd known better than to get involved with Triss. He had two little kids to protect from loss and disappointment. They had enough to contend with in life without a mom. He'd do well to keep that at the forefront of his mind.

NINE

Triss was crazy. And Hunter was furious. He'd been on his way to Harmony for his shift when Bryan called to let him know that Triss had gone on a run.

Hunter sped down the road, hands tight on the wheel. What was she thinking? Bryan said she'd insisted it was her routine and she'd refused to let fear change her routine. Well, fear didn't have to change her routine, but common sense did.

Up ahead, the stadium came into view, and he slowed, turning the corner into the parking lot. He pulled up next to Bryan's car and got out.

Bryan unrolled his window.

"Where is she?"

Bryan pointed to the bleachers, and Hunter turned to look, confused for a minute until he spotted a shadow of a figure jogging up the bleachers, a spot of a flashlight along with her.

"Seriously?"

"She has her Mace, her gun and her flashlight, and she didn't like being followed."

Hunter shook his head. "I'll take it from here."

"All right. Don't freeze. See you tonight."

Bryan closed the window and pulled away from the empty lot, and Hunter headed toward the bleachers, tamping down his anger and trying to decide the best course of action. If she was going to insist on predawn runs, she'd need to agree to protection.

He strode around the chain-link fence to an opening, walking through just in time to see Triss reach the bottom of the bleachers and head up again. He leaned against the railing, the feel of cold metal seeping through his jacket as he readied his argument for when she turned and headed to the bottom. Only, he was sidetracked by one thought: she was phenomenal. Wearing dark black running tights and a long-sleeve hoodie, she charged up the high bleachers without a break in stride, the echo of her footsteps pounding on metal in a quick rhythm. She'd wrapped her thick hair into a tight bun, a wide headband covering her ears, and white puffs of breath were visible as she reached the top of the bleachers. Then she turned, barely slowing, and made quick work of the descent, a mini flashlight focused at her feet.

She didn't realize Hunter was there until she was near the bottom, and she finally slowed, her face cast in shadows.

"You don't have to freeze out here with me," she said. "I've got two more sets, and I'm done."

With that, she turned on her heel and started up again. Well, they were already at the stadium, so Hunter figured he'd let her finish her workout. Then, he'd make it perfectly clear why she would have to adjust her workout routine for a while.

She finished her workout within minutes and finally stepped off the bleachers. "I told you you didn't have to stay out here with me."

Hunter didn't bother to point out the fallacy in that statement, or how it went against every Shield proto-col. Instead, he shoved off from the railing and led the way toward the parking lot. They could talk on the way to Harmony.

"I'll meet you at Harmony," Triss said as they stepped around the gate, and she started a fast jog.

"Hold on a minute," Hunter said, running to catch up with her. "It's a two-mile trek. It's pitch-black out here. Let me drive you."

Hunter kept pace with her, glad he'd taken her advice and dressed in khakis and a dry-fit polo, but his shoes weren't made for running two miles at Triss's pace.

"I'll remember to wear my sneakers tomorrow."

She slowed to a stop under a corner streetlight, her breathing coming in short huffs. "I run alone," she told him. "You don't need to worry about me." She lifted her right hand, where she had strapped a palm-sized bottle of Mace. "Also, I'm carrying."

"That Mace won't do much against a car that runs you off the road. And try reaching that gun if someone jumps out and grabs you from behind. This is insanity, Triss. Either let me drive you, or I guess I'm running next to you the rest of the way."

Her full lips flattened in frustration, and she looked like she might take off running again. Instead, not say-ing a word, she started toward the parking lot, her focus set on his truck.

She got there ahead of him, hopped inside and closed the door. Didn't slam it, like he'd expected her to, though she'd seemed mad enough to attempt a door slam. Hunter got in the driver's side and pulled out of the lot. He shouldn't feel bad. He was only doing his job. Even Triss should see that. She was a Shield agent. She had to know that they'd never let an endangered client go on a run alone. But he could see by the rigid set of her profile that they weren't on the same page here.

"We're going to need to compromise," Triss said finally after a long silence.

"One word," Hunter said. "Treadmill."

"Not happening."

"It's not forever. Hopefully, we'll get this situation nailed in a week or so, and we can get you back to your routine, and then—"

"I'd rather not run for the next week than run on a treadmill, going nowhere."

"Well, that's even easier," Hunter said. "Take a week off. You could use it right about now."

"Do me a favor, Hunter. Think of me as a client. We help our clients live and function safely in daily life. They don't change all their routines."

She had a point there. "But we have more resources with most of our clients," Hunter responded. "We'd never let someone go running with just one agent on security detail."

"Circumstances are different. I'm a trained agent, too." She glanced at him, fire in her dark eyes. "I'm not going to stop running my route, and I'm not in the market for a running partner."

"So, you want me to follow at a snail's pace in my car every day?"

"If you feel the need."

Hunter sighed and unlocked the doors. "You win."

Hunter was probably upset with her for canceling on the party at the last minute. He'd only responded to her text yesterday with an "okay." If he was upset, though, that could be for the best, she told herself. Hunter would see that she wasn't the kind of person who could be a reliable mother to his kids, and he would want nothing to do with her. Problem solved.

Predictably, Hunter had caught up with her before she even got out of the parking lot. It was a lonely stretch of road on a Sunday morning, and she had to admit that the headlights from his vehicle following her put her at ease. Granted, the sight of a slow truck following a lone female jogger might prompt a suspicious passerby to call police, but the cars were few and far between, the drivers either disinterested or distracted.

To cool down, Triss usually jogged slowly on the way to Harmony, but she ran faster with Hunter following in his truck, knowing it was torturous to drive at five miles an hour for two miles.

She didn't want to admit it, but the run was tough on her. Logically, she knew that her two hospital visits and her lack of sleep were to blame, but still she pushed herself, her calves still burning from her bleacher runs, her lungs on fire from her sustained speed.

Suddenly, just behind her, Hunter laid on his horn. Triss gasped, turning toward him in time to see the car.

It seemed to come out of nowhere, headlights off and pedal to the metal. And it was coming straight for her!

For a paralyzed moment, Triss froze, unsure which way to take cover. And then Hunter made the decision for her, as he pulled up next to her and screamed at her to get off the road.

She lunged onto the grass beyond the shoulder as Hunter maneuvered his truck in front of the oncoming car.

Tires screeched, the smaller car spinning out before nicking the front bumper of the truck. The sound of the crash echoed through the surrounding trees before the driver, shrouded in shadows, peeled away from the scene.

Hunter straightened out the truck and pulled up next to Triss. "Hop in."

She did so quickly, yanking on her seat belt with a trembling hand.

"You okay?" Hunter asked, his gaze probing the darkness to assess her.

"Just shook me up." She turned to look behind them, but the car had disappeared around the bend.

"Who do we know with a gray sedan?" Hunter asked, pulling onto the road to drive the last quarter mile back to Harmony.

"I don't know, but it shouldn't be hard to find out." She held up her phone, a grainy photo of the license plate filling the screen.

He grinned, impressed. "Good job. In the meantime— treadmill."

"Right."

* * *

Triss was correct in her prediction. It didn't take long to run the plates and discover that the car belonged to Kristy Ingles. The vehicle—and its keys—were missing. But Kristy was sound asleep when Triss and Hunter went banging on her door, her confusion evident. They banged on everyone else's door, too, but everyone who lived at Harmony was accounted for. It wasn't long before the car was located, parked in a cul-de-sac of an adjoining neighborhood, close enough for its driver to scale the fence and sneak into Harmony without anyone knowing.

Except for the security cameras.

And that's how Triss and Hunter ended up in the security office, scrolling through footage to identify who had stolen Kristy's car.

All they found were three sightings of a shadowed figure wearing bulky clothes and a dark hat in the very early hours—and no way to identify him because only half of the new cameras had been installed. In fact, two of them hadn't been switched on and connected to the monitoring system.

"First thing on the agenda today—finish installing the cameras," Hunter said, frustration in his voice.

"I can help after ten," Triss offered. "I promised George that I'd go with him to church this morning."

"Church, huh?" He turned toward her, not making a move to leave the quiet office yet.

He knew well her aversion to churches. Three weeks ago, Walter's funeral had marked the first time she'd entered a church in nearly seven years. As far as she knew, Hunter wasn't a churchgoer, either.

"The chapel's right on the property."

"Just surprised you agreed."

"Moment of weakness," she said, reaching for her door latch. "George's been lonely lately. He was good friends with Frank and Walter. He was all teary-eyed. I don't handle tears well." She stood. "Guess I should go grab a shower."

"About yesterday," Hunter said, not making a move to leave.

She paused, surprised at the turn of the conversation. "I'm sorry. She wasn't too upset, was she?"

She could tell by the look in his eyes that Josie had been upset, but he was too kind to say it.

"She got over it when I told her she was going to get to help bathe a baby elephant."

To be fair, she hadn't thought Josie would be all that disappointed. Apparently, she'd been wrong.

"I feel terrible."

Hunter ran a hand through his hair and stared at the monitors for a moment before returning his attention to her. "I wasn't trying to make you feel guilty about it."

Too late, Triss thought. But she probably deserved it.

"I want to know the truth," he said, his eyes searching for answers she wasn't ready to give him.

"I told you I was tired. I shouldn't have bailed, though, and—"

"The other truth."

The air in the office stilled as Triss looked into the

face of the only person who had ever been able to see right through her facade.

She wanted to deny the other truth, insist that he believe the no-sleep excuse, but something in his eyes broke down her defenses.

For the first time in years, she wanted to tell someone—no, tell *him*. He'd see, then, what was holding her back. He was an honorable guy, empathetic to the extreme. He'd respect her wishes and stay away, and she would finally be able to confide her loss to someone—even if that meant he would never look at her the same way again.

"I've seen you work forty-eight-hour shifts," he said quietly, his gaze probing. "I've seen you power through a week of full-time work and part-time school against doctor's orders after a concussion. I've watched you come back at one hundred percent just one week after a life-threatening stabbing. I know you were tired yesterday. But I want to know what it is you're not telling me."

She hadn't considered telling anyone in years, and now the words sat, uncertain, on the tip of her tongue and the edge of her heart. "Hunter, I—"

A door squeaked open, and she swiveled around as Adam walked in. He stopped short in the doorway, his gaze moving between the two. "Everything okay?" he asked.

"We were just checking something out," Hunter said.

Triss noticed again Adam's pale face and the dark circles rimming his eyes. "Are *you* okay?" she asked, taking advantage of the moment, relieved that they'd been interrupted, her senses coming back to her. Her secret remained safe.

To her surprise, Adam's eyes glazed over and he shook his head. "My mom was diagnosed with cancer a few weeks ago." He cleared his throat, his cheeks ruddy.

Triss's suspicions fled, compassion taking over. They spent the next hour with Adam, and before Triss and Hunter left the security office, they had convinced him to start seeing a counselor to help deal with his grief. They'd also devised a plan to package Creekside Manor dinner leftovers once a week to send over to Adam's family. Barb often made too much and hated to see food go to waste.

Outside, the sun was rising on another cold fall day. Hunter cocked his head to the side, disappointment drawing the corners of his mouth downward. "Adam saved you this time," he said. "But I'm not letting this go."

"I wish you would," she said, the words coming out in a near whisper as they entered Creekside Manor, which was bustling with activity as most of the residents prepared to go to church.

"Not a chance," he responded, determination in his voice.

The words were more promise than threat, and as Triss made her way to her apartment to prepare for the day, she couldn't help but wonder what would happen if she told him her secret? What if she just came clean? To Hunter, to Luke, to *everyone*? The freedom in that idea encouraged her, but she wasn't sure she was ready. Didn't know if she ever would be.

TEN

Triss's apartment door swung open, and she appeared wearing a cream long-sleeve blouse of what looked like the softest satin paired with gray dress pants and heels. She looked ready to go to work, except for her hair. She'd straightened it but had left it loose instead of wrapping it up in a ponytail. Shiny locks spilled nearly halfway down her back.

"Ready?" Hunter asked.

She shrugged. "I guess so." She looked ruefully at her pants. "I don't own any dresses. They might not even let me in."

"Wishful thinking," Hunter said with humor. They walked down the hallway and outside into the chilly, sunny morning. Ahead of them, others were already on their way to the chapel, most chatting with one another and making their way leisurely. Hunter identified with Triss's lack of enthusiasm. He'd grown up going to church, but since moving out and starting his own life, he'd only really ever been a holiday churchgoer.

He'd always believed in God, but had never bought

into the idea of God as an approachable friend who was involved in every aspect of his life. Instead, he had a general impression of a God who watched from afar and intervened only occasionally, and usually unpredictably.

They passed Silverwood and Emerald, and then turned left on the paved walkway, the chapel coming into view. It sat like a sacred sanctuary at the edge of the property, shaded by maples in their fall glory, the trickle of a narrow stream sounding in the woods beyond. He'd taken several patrolling loops around the property over the past couple of days, and he had to admit it was a peaceful place. The chapel itself was small and quaint, built with white bricks and topped with a rather large bell that gently rang each hour. It could barely be heard at the front of the Harmony community, but now it began to ring for the 9:00 a.m. service, its peaceful chiming echoing over the area.

George was waiting by the entrance, smiling as Triss approached. He wore black dress pants and a suit jacket with a bright yellow tie. He handed Triss a Bible. "You made it. I brought you one of my extras," he said, then glanced at Hunter. "Didn't think to bring two."

"We can share," Hunter replied, feeling a little sorry for the guy. If he thought that opening a Bible and sitting through a church service was going to change either Triss's or Hunter's life, he was going to come away sorely disappointed. And, according to Triss, he was already struggling with depression.

"Thanks, George," Triss said, tucking the Bible under her arm and linking her other arm with his as they walked through the double doors. "Show us the way."

Predictably, George ushered them directly to the front, choosing seats in the second row of pews. Hunter glanced around the congregation as the pews began to fill in. He'd rather stand near the entrance and keep a view of everyone from there, but he knew that Adam would be stationed there, and it was more important that Hunter stick with Triss.

Kaye sat at the piano, a soft look of contentment on her face as she played through the familiar hymn of "Amazing Grace," and then faded the music out as a young man in a fitted gray suit with a blue tie made his way to the front.

"Good morning, friends!" he said with a welcoming smile. "Join me in the Lord's Prayer."

Hunter found himself reciting the prayer by rote, the familiar verses tumbling out, despite not having repeated them in years. Next to him, Triss quietly spoke the words as well, which also surprised him. Even though her brother seemed to live by a deep faith, Triss had never given any indication that she'd felt connected to religion in any way.

He settled against the hard oak pew, resisting the urge to drape his arm over Triss's shoulders. A sense of peace seemed to wash over him within the walls of a church. It was something he'd always noticed about church growing up, and when he went with the kids for Christmas and Easter. He imagined that peace was tied to childhood traditions and had never thought much of it.

The congregation sang hymns from traditional hard-backed hymnals to Kaye's solo piano accompaniment, and then the young pastor launched into his sermon. Hunter, as per usual, zoned out. He wished again that they were sitting closer to the back. He wanted to observe the occupants of the room, but from his vantage point, he could only keep an eye on a dozen or so of the churchgoers.

Next to him, Triss was opening the borrowed Bible, flipping to the New Testament in search of the verses the pastor had posted on the projector screen.

She found the book of John, turning the delicate pages gently until she'd found the right chapter and verse. So, she knew her way around the Bible as well as the Lord's Prayer. Interesting.

Absently, he read the verse—*I am the light of the world: he that followeth Me shall not walk in darkness, but shall have the light of life.* Something stirred in his heart at the words, but he ignored it. He'd never spent much time pondering verses from the Bible; had never found much of what he *had* read to be applicable.

The pastor continued with his sermon, which seemed to revolve around the theme of bringing darkness to light. Bringing secrets out so they lose their power. The message didn't apply to Hunter. He was a face-value kind of guy, and about as secretive as his gregarious two-year-old.

A while later, he realized, belatedly, that everyone had bowed their heads and the sermon was coming to a close through prayer. Dutifully, he bowed his head, but kept his eyes open, always on alert.

Still, he tuned into the words as the pastor prayed against the pull of darkness in the world. It was a prayer of blessing, a prayer of hope. But Hunter saw a flash of his life.

Darkness.

But, no. He would never describe his life as dark. Despite his wife's death and his kids missing out on a mother, he was fairly content—even happy—with his life. Why those words struck his heart so sharply, he couldn't identify. Was it possible to live in darkness and not realize it?

A teardrop landed on the open page in Triss's lap, and she swiped it away, swiftly closing the Bible. He glanced at her profile, but her hair hid her face as she prayed, and he couldn't detect her emotions.

The pastor ended the prayer and finally dismissed everyone.

Triss stood, the only sign of emotion a barely detectable glossiness in her eyes.

He followed her as she walked out with George and stopped to chat with several residents on their way. Once they got to the walkway, she held out the Bible. "Thanks for letting me borrow it," she said.

George waved it away. "It's yours. Keep it." He waved hurriedly at Mack, calling out his name. "I'll be seeing you."

Triss held on to the Bible and kept walking, but she veered off the walkway toward the creek that ran by the church.

As she neared the creek, she slipped off her heels and slowed her pace. Hunter followed silently, suspecting that whatever was happening would be a turning point for them.

He stood next to her, hands in his pockets to keep himself from tugging her to his side.

A cardinal sat on a nearly bare limb of a tree across from them, the creek clear and moving swiftly over pebbles and craggy rocks. It was a whimsical scene, but when Triss finally turned to face him, he knew that whatever she was about to say would not be light and fairy-tale-like.

"I'm sorry I canceled on Josie's party yesterday," she said. "And I'm sorry I dropped out of your lives this summer." She paused, pressing her lips together, vivid grief in her eyes.

Without thinking, he reached for her, unable to watch her stand so heartbroken and alone, but she stepped back.

"Don't." She said the word sadly, almost hopelessly, and he suspected that she wouldn't pull away if he tried again, but he dropped his arms and waited instead, giving her the time and space to say whatever else she needed to say.

"I've been keeping a secret for six years, and I think it's killing me. It's the reason why you and I will never work, and it's only fair that I tell you now. So you'll understand. And so, maybe, I can start to move on."

A cool wind ruffled against Triss's too-thin blouse, and she hugged George's Bible to her chest as if it would somehow give her warmth. Or strength. She'd started now, and there was no going back.

"The baby clothes and toys you found in my apartment," she began, watching Hunter's reaction closely. "I bought them for my daughter."

Only a slight widening of his eyes showed that he had heard. But he stood still, waiting patiently, like he always did, and Triss took a deep breath and told him her story.

The words tumbled out like the running water of the stream, cleansing and freeing her heart of the secret she'd held tightly for too long.

He listened without saying a word until she had to eventually turn to the stream to finish her story, unable to bear the way he watched her—the compassion in his eyes, the way he shoved his hands in his pockets, she knew, so he wouldn't try to hug her again.

"A couple of months after the adoption, I decided to come home," she said, finishing her story. "I didn't want to tell Luke. He would have helped me raise her. But he'd spent years raising Cal and me already. I couldn't do that to him."

She was silent for a moment, letting Hunter digest the story, and he finally spoke.

"What did you tell him?"

"I just knocked on the door one evening, and he hugged me so hard I almost couldn't breathe." She smiled, tears leaking out at the memory. "I asked him not to ask me questions, and I promised I would never disappear again."

"And he accepted that?" Hunter asked, surprise in his voice.

"He tried a few times, but I shut him down. I think he was afraid I'd run again. I used his fear to my advantage. Remember—I was sixteen. Not exactly thinking about anyone but myself."

She took a breath and turned to Hunter. "I love y-your kids, your little family." Her heart raced as she nearly slipped and told him she loved him. Her eyes flooded again and she pressed the tears away, annoyed. "I haven't cried in years. I think these funerals over the past weeks opened up the dam."

"You've got a few years of tears built up," he said softly.

"Crying is useless, though."

"Some call it cleansing." His eyes searched hers. "You were saying…you love my kids?" A gentle smile played on his lips.

"I do. But it's too painful, Hunter." The tears fell freely now, and she couldn't stop them, her voice hitching as she struggled to explain. "I wanted to die after I said goodbye to my daughter. I had never loved someone so much. I couldn't imagine living the rest of my life without her, and I felt so ashamed. One night, I went to the Chesapeake Bay Bridge. I almost jumped, but a passerby stopped me. When I finally came home, I started drinking. Finally understood what had driven my mom to drinking and drugs. Sometimes, there's so much pain, you just want out. But one morning, I woke up and decided to start over again."

"Meaning?"

"I laid out goals for myself and made a plan to achieve them. I only let myself think about my daughter for one week per year—the week of her birthday. I would buy her a gift for each birthday."

"The gifts I found in the chest in your living room."

She nodded, swallowing past the urge to break down and weep. "On her birthday, I would always say a prayer for her and put the gift in the chest, and then I would close the chest and refuse to think about her for the next year."

"Survival skills," Hunter remarked, watching her. She could tell he still didn't understand what her daughter had to do with their relationship.

"Josie and my daughter are only two weeks apart in age, Hunter. Every milestone reminds me of what I walked away from. I can't do that for the rest of my life. I'm not built that way. I won't survive it." Her voice broke on the words, but she added one final, desperate plea. "Please, don't ask me to."

He was silent for a long moment, and then he reached a hand toward her, his knuckles gently brushing the dampness from her cheeks.

Warmth spiraled through her from the touch, and she forced herself to keep her feet firmly planted and not step into what she knew would be his welcome embrace.

He dropped his hand and shifted on his feet, his expression falling into one of sad acceptance. "I won't ask you to," he finally said, his voice thick with emotion. "But I won't pretend I don't wish things could be different between us."

She nodded, her heart all at once relieved and achingly sad. "I know." She turned from the creek, shoving her feet into her heels. Her toes were numb from cold, and the shoes didn't do much to warm her up. "But now you know why."

She started toward the walkway and he walked beside her, hands in his pockets. "Will you ever tell Luke?" he asked, and her heart tripped at the thought.

"I think I have to now," she said.

"What are you afraid of?"

"That he'll tell me he would have helped me raise her. That I made the wrong choice."

"Do you think it was the wrong choice?"

"Sometimes."

"I think it was brave, Triss," he said as they walked, and the sun suddenly felt warm on her face. "At barely sixteen, to run away and have a baby without any support system, to choose adoption, to come home and start a new life despite all you'd been through—that takes an unbelievable amount of courage and strength."

His words flowed over her like the healing rays of sunshine, the affirmation that she had gone so many years unable to accept.

"Maybe, one day, you can connect with her again," he offered as they approached Creekside.

She'd thought about it each year. Had drafted and redrafted an email to the adoption agency. The adoptive parents had hoped for an open adoption. She'd made the decision to keep it closed, believing it would best for everyone. She'd regretted it ever since.

"Maybe," she said noncommittally, because she was afraid of that, too. Afraid of finding out her daughter was unhappy, unloved, alone. That Triss had actually made the worst choice she could have made, even out of the desperate hope and desire to do the right thing and give her daughter the best chance.

"Roman will need some time to get someone to take over my shift," Hunter said as he reached for the door. "I'll talk to him after the holiday. Hopefully, we'll catch this lunatic by then."

Triss nodded. "Good." It was right and simple. The best way to break their ties with one another, and she knew it. But it didn't make it any less painful. She'd known, however, that Hunter wouldn't fight her. He was too good of a man, too honorable. He would accept her decision, especially now that she'd made it perfectly clear and he could understand her reasoning. She should feel only relief, but she felt strangely empty.

ELEVEN

Drained from finally telling someone about her daughter, all Triss wanted to do was head to her apartment and be alone for a while, but as soon as she walked into Harmony, she was pulled into a discussion by Sissy and Kaye about the week's festivities. There would be pie-baking and Thanksgiving tree making, and Kaye suggested that Hunter bring his kids to the Thanksgiving eve festivities. Zach's family was coming into town to lead a sing-along as they put up the facility's Christmas tree and strung popcorn, and all of the planning and holiday excitement forced Triss's thoughts away from her daughter and Hunter—and how much she was going to miss him and his kids.

Eventually, she was able to slip away from the group and change into a pair of track pants and a hoodie. She tied her hair into a big bun and shoved on a pair of sneakers before heading to lunch. Her stomach rumbled, but she couldn't decide if she was actually hungry or just anxious and emotional. She'd been moved by the pastor's sermon earlier, and she didn't regret telling

Hunter about her daughter. In fact, she did feel lighter after confessing her secret and seeing how warmly it was received. She'd go to Luke's house tonight and tell him, too. Get it over with so she didn't have to keep thinking about it.

But she just felt tired and a little nauseous, truth be told. She wasn't used to letting herself feel so deeply. She'd spent so many years stuffing down her thoughts and fears and regrets that when she'd finally started to let it come out, she was physically exhausted by it.

The scent of chicken tortilla soup filled the hallway, and Triss was tempted to fill a big bowl. She didn't dare, though, and headed straight to the kitchen to grab one of the premade chicken-and-rice bowls from the fridge. She heated the meal in the microwave and then walked into the dining hall, joining a group of several of her friends.

"You look terrible," Riley announced before realizing how rude she'd sounded. "I mean—"

"I'm aware," Triss said, cutting her off. She wasn't exactly living her best week.

She took a bite of the chicken and rice, her stomach queasy. The dish was weirdly sweet—or Triss was in a lot of turmoil. She swallowed and washed down the bite with water, setting her fork on the table. Maybe she'd make herself some toast a little later.

Conversations swirled around her and she scanned the room, wondering who had followed her that morning, who had been lying in wait with Kristy's stolen car to try to…what? Scare her? Run her down? Why?

She zeroed in on some of the conversations—Kristy

and Zach talking about the damaged car; Hunter and George debating best holiday pies; Kaye and Courtney setting up their meeting.

George leaned forward, his voice lowering. "Between you and me, I think she's a little self-important."

Triss held back a laugh. Courtney had confidence, and she liked to tell everyone about her endeavors. Her research project was an endless conversation. They would all be glad when she finished interviewing her last subject—Kaye.

"At least it's an interesting topic, right?" she asked. "Something about combating loneliness in the elderly population."

George rolled his eyes and leaned back in his chair. "That kind of research is only interesting to the younger generation. We aren't lonely. We're tired of being social." He grinned. "We're antisocial, and we've earned the right to be."

It was Triss's turn to roll her eyes. "Whatever you say, George." She saw the loneliness firsthand. It was shocking how few of the residents had regular visitors, especially considering how many of them had children who lived close by. She'd like to think that she would have been a presence in her mom's life, if she would have lived, but she didn't know enough to judge.

"There she goes again," George said suddenly, and Triss turned in her seat to see what he was looking at.

Iris was slumped forward in her seat, her cheek half on the table, half on the plate.

Triss jumped out of her seat and ran to the woman,

shaking her awake. What was up with her narcolepsy lately?

"It's just her condition," George said, then swallowed another spoonful of soup.

But was it? Triss had a flashback to Iris in the ocean. Was someone still after her? Hunter appeared at her side, and Triss leaned forward and shook Iris's shoulder, relieved when the woman jerked up into a sitting position.

"I fell asleep again," she said, stating the obvious.

"Don't you have a medication for this?" Triss asked. "Did it stop working?"

"I ran out," Iris said, her accent soft, her expression perplexed. "Can't think of how, unless some spilled and I didn't realize. Too early to get a refill."

"It's a liquid?" Triss asked, red flags shooting up in her mind. The previous day, she'd asked Iris about her bank accounts, but Iris kept meticulous records and had found nothing out of the ordinary. With no clues as to why someone would target Iris, Triss had started to second-guess herself.

"Yes." She shrugged. "I wonder if the pharmacist cheated me."

"Maybe you can talk to your doctor and get a refill, anyway?"

Iris frowned. "It's a real hassle to get it."

"I could drive you," Triss started to suggest, but Iris was already shaking her head.

"It's a controlled medication."

Triss stilled. "What is the medicine you're taking, Iris?"

"It's called Xyrem. Works like a dream."

Xyrem, the drug Dr. O'Neill had mentioned.

"For your narcolepsy?" she asked, certain she must be wrong.

Iris nodded. "Yes, why?"

Triss's mind raced back to her lab results and the question of how Iris's prescription medication could have ended up in her food or drink.

"It's a drug prescribed sometimes for narcolepsy," Courtney chimed in. "But Iris is right—getting a refill ahead of schedule probably wouldn't work. It's a controlled drug."

"Controlled, why?" Triss asked, but she had a feeling she already knew.

"It's basically a form of GHB," Courtney said. "Pretty dangerous when it's misused."

"Well, it does its job for me," Iris said, and she stood to leave. "I think I'll take a little nap at my place." As she walked out of the room, Harrison appeared in the entrance, his stance alert, his focus urgent.

"Got a minute?" He gestured for her to follow him.

She excused herself, tossed her dish in the trash and followed Harrison out of the room, Hunter catching up in seconds.

"Did you catch all that?" she asked Hunter as they walked to her apartment with Harrison.

He nodded. "You calling Goodson, or should I?"

"I'll do it after we see what Harrison has to say."

There was no doubt in her mind that someone had gotten into Iris's medication and used it on Triss the other night. Had the same person seen the theft's effect on Iris and taken advantage of her sleep spells to toss her overboard? If so, why? Who had a motive here? She needed to find some way to convince the police to seriously start investigating the four deaths before there were more deaths to investigate.

As soon as she'd shut the door to her apartment, she turned to find Harrison standing in front of her, his expression serious.

"Someone's been looking into the use of coolant as a method for poisoning," he said. "We need to check the cameras in the kitchen."

Her stomach rolled, but she mostly felt fine. She'd only taken a small bite. But it *had* tasted strange…

"It was under Don's account this time," he said. "But I don't think it was him. The time stamp is from two days ago, late into the night—close to midnight, and before the new cameras were activated."

"Don's in bed by eight most nights," Triss pointed out, trying to ignore the rising nausea.

"I got that impression."

"Do you feel okay?" Hunter asked her.

"Kind of queasy, to be honest. My food tasted off."

The two men stared at her, alarm in their expressions.

"I only took one bite. I'm sure it's okay."

"We should get you to a doctor," Hunter said, his eyes serious.

"I'm fine," Triss insisted. "But this is getting out of hand. We've got to figure out who's behind it all."

Hunter looked like he might argue, but then Harrison spoke up.

"I'll put in a call to Poison Control and ask some questions when we're done here," he offered.

The idea seemed to appease Hunter, and he nodded

his agreement. "First order of business will be to pull footage from the cameras, though my guess is the coolant was added to your food before the cameras went up. Maybe even the night of the internet search." Pulling out a folded piece of paper from his pocket, he motioned for the two of them to join him in the living room. As they sat around the coffee table, he opened the paper and set it in front of them.

"This is the list of people who were on the ferry. I crossed out the least likely culprits—the captain and crew, anyone not related to Harmony."

Triss silently counted. "That leaves twenty-six people."

"We need to go through this list systematically and narrow it down. If we can first figure out who could have committed all of the crimes, then we can look at possible motives."

"Speaking of which, I wonder if we could go around the police and ask the families some questions," Triss suggested. Her stomach churned, but she ignored it, willing the nausea away.

"Roman was trying that avenue," Hunter said. "The families have all been advised to speak with no one but police."

"So the deaths *are* being investigated," Triss said, somewhat reassured that they weren't on their own in this mess—even if it sure felt like they were. "Anything else, Harrison, before I call Officer Goodson?"

He shook his head. "Not yet. I'll keep you posted."

Several police cruisers sat in front of Creekside Manor two hours later, and the facility was eerily quiet.

Everyone had been asked to stay in their apartments while police investigated. Food from the dining hall had been bagged to be tested, including the premade meals Triss had waiting for her in the fridge. Whatever she'd eaten had made her pretty sick. She'd thrown up twice but refused to go to the hospital because she felt better within a fairly short period. She was visiting with Kaye and Sissy right now, and Hunter settled into the leather couch, his mind flashing back two years, as he followed the ambulance that carried his wife, having tucked a sleeping four-year-old Josie and newborn Levi into car seats and followed with no time to call anyone to watch the kids. By the time he'd arrived inside the hospital, it was too late. His wife had died.

The doctors tried for a long time to revive her, but nothing could be done. Too many times over the past days, Hunter had imagined he was too late for Triss. She had made herself clear today, and he was prepared to step out of her life. But he wasn't prepared for her life to be taken. He wanted nothing but the best for her, even if that didn't include him.

He thought about the story she had told him, the tears she had shed by the creek that morning, the daughter she had courageously chosen to relinquish for adoption. If anything, her story had made him love her more, which made the idea of losing her that much harder.

Tonight he'd talk to Roman and make sure someone they could all trust would take his place at Harmony after Thanksgiving. He'd never be able to honor her wishes to let her live her life without him unless he turned and physically walked away.

Restless, he stood and started down the hall, but the officer stopped him. "Sorry—we're still finishing up in the dining hall. I'll let you know when it's okay to enter. We're planning to go door-to-door for interviews, and everyone has been instructed to stay on-site until interviewed."

"Any progress on looking into the four deaths of residents?" Hunter asked.

"Two were cremated," the officer said. "We've started talks with family members of the others, but without concrete evidence, it's a tough sell for them to allow us to exhume the bodies and pursue an investigation. We're working on gathering evidence for some warrants."

Goodson's partner called him, and he shrugged apologetically. "Sit tight for a few."

Hunter couldn't sit tight. He had someone in mind to talk to, and he walked down the hall to knock on Iris's door. She opened it and invited him inside, her white eyebrows furrowed in deep concern. He signed her visitor log before she even had a chance to hand it to him, and kindly refused the offered seat.

"I won't stay long," he said. "I just wanted to ask you about your prescription for Xyrem."

Confusion swept over her features and she cocked her head to the side. "What about it?"

"You said that you're out of the pills prematurely?"

"It's a liquid, but yes. I thought I had several doses left the last time I took it."

"Where do you keep the prescription bottle?" Hunter asked.

"Right in my purse, always," she said emphatically. "Sometimes I forget to take it in the morning, and when I remember I'm already at breakfast. Hate to come all the way back to my apartment for it."

"Did you throw away the empty bottle?"

"Not yet. The pharmacy's number is on the bottle, and I keep meaning to call…"

Hunter tried not to get too excited, knowing her hands had been all over the bottle and likely had destroyed any fingerprints that may have been on it. He didn't for one minute think that Iris could be the culprit.

"Why are you asking these questions?"

"It's a long story, Iris," he said, not sure how much information he should share with her. He quickly sent a text to Officer Goodson asking him to come to Iris's apartment. "I'll tell you all the details later, okay?"

"Am I in trouble?" she asked, wringing her hands together in her lap.

"No, no, you're not in trouble," he said. "We think you could help us, actually."

The officer tapped on the door, and Hunter explained that the empty prescription bottle was still inside Iris's purse.

Iris was already grabbing her purse and reaching for the bottle before either man could stop her.

"Not sure why you need it, but you're welcome to it. Just let me copy the phone number on it."

Officer Goodson pulled on latex gloves and grabbed the bottle from her, holding it out so she could jot down the number. He then slipped it into an evidence bag, and they thanked Iris and left.

"I'll have my guy rush processing on this," the officer said, holding the bag up to the light, as if he could identify the culprit's prints by staring hard enough and under enough light.

But just before he dropped his arm, Hunter noticed something. "Wait."

The officer held it up to the light in the hallway, and Hunter looked closer. "There's a hair stuck to it," he said.

Officer Goodson stared for a moment, his eyes widening. "You're right. Short, black and looks like—"

"Bleached on the ends."

"Only person around here I know with hair like that is Zach," Hunter said, his pulse racing. Could it be that easy? Had Zach left a hair with his fingerprint? The two looked closely at the bottle through the bag, clearly seeing the single strand of hair, which was seemingly stuck under the cap of the prescription bottle.

"Looks like Zach is my next interview," Officer Goodson said, and Hunter pointed down the hallway. When they arrived at Zach's door, Hunter knocked and stood waiting, reminding himself to be professional. But when Zach opened the door, all he wanted to do was slug him in the face.

He resisted the urge as Officer Goodson greeted him and asked if they could talk.

Zach led them to the living room, his perfectly styled hair gelled and standing high. He'd done nothing to decorate his apartment and seemed nervous to have the men there.

After a series of questions that led to no interesting

information, Zach finally frowned. "Do you think I have something to do with what's been going on around here?" he asked.

"Everyone will be interviewed tonight," Officer Goodson said, skating around the question.

Zach nodded. "Well, I don't have anything to hide. You can even search my place if it'll make you feel better."

Hunter couldn't believe his ears. Was Zach opening up his place to a warrantless search? He resisted the urge to advise him to get a lawyer first. If he wasn't guilty, nothing would be found. No harm, no foul.

Officer Goodson was extremely careful about the search, recording Zach's permission and reading him his rights, but Zach didn't waver, was adamant—almost too adamant—that they wouldn't find anything.

The officer called in his partner and another officer to help him conduct the search while Hunter sat with Zach in the living room, suspicious but certain the search would yield nothing.

After several long minutes, Officer Goodson appeared. "You have diabetes?" he asked, and Zach frowned.

"What? No."

"You have a friend or family member with diabetes who stays here?"

"No…what are you talking about?"

The officer held out a small bag with what appeared to be several insulin shots.

Zach shot up out of his seat. "They're not mine."

"They were under your bathroom cabinet, behind

rolls of toilet paper," the officer said. "You sure you don't know who they belong to?"

Zach shook his head, but he no longer looked calm and collected, as fear entered his expression.

"I don't know where that came from, but I think I want you to stop searching my place. I think I need to ask you to get a warrant to finish the search," he said, his voice shaking.

Hunter shook his head. Had the kid not anticipated the police would find what he'd been hiding? He thought about the insulin and Walter Tompkins. Zach would have had access to the man. Could he have been counting on benefiting from an inheritance because he was dating Walter's granddaughter? And the Xyrem made sense. With his medical background, he could easily put ideas together on sinister ways to misuse medication.

Anger rose up hot, and Hunter knew if he stayed a moment longer in the apartment, he couldn't be trusted to keep his hands off the guy without risking jail time. Instead, he left the apartment and went in search of Triss, adrenaline pumping and his temper simmering.

TWELVE

The scent of pumpkin pie permeated all of Creekside Manor. Triss sat in a recliner in the commons, tediously stringing needle and thread through popcorn to decorate the tree the residents would help erect the next day, after Thanksgiving dinner. Soft Christmas music played, and residents and staff alike had filled the room, stringing popcorn and writing their blessings on leaves for the Thanksgiving tree poster Brandon had affixed to a far wall. By all accounts, Triss should feel lighter and full of new hope. She had survived what could have been several deadly attacks, Zach had been arrested, the deaths at Harmony were being investigated and she'd sent the email she'd been rewriting for half a dozen years.

Only, her heart felt strangely heavy. Roman had pulled his team from Harmony starting today, all evidence pointing to Zach despite the confounding lack of motive. Stella had insisted, and he couldn't exactly force their way onto the property. She'd claimed she would hire extra security officers at a fraction of the cost, but thanked them kindly for their service.

Triss would see Hunter and the kids tonight, but she wasn't sure when after that. Her internship with the FBI would begin in January, and she'd be leaving Shield officially. Her brother couldn't be happier, and she had to admit to being a bit relieved herself. Her job at Shield had ended up being much more dangerous than she'd ever anticipated. At the FBI, she'd be getting hands-on training in forensic-scene investigation, and she'd be even closer to finally achieving her career goals.

Still, that excitement was shadowed by the sorrow she felt about saying goodbye to Hunter and the kids tonight. And also the unanswered questions she had about Zach.

"What a thing, huh?" Kaye asked, neatly threading her needle through another popcorn puff. "Zach. I would never have guessed."

"I still don't understand it," Triss said. "Then again, even if someone gave me a plausible motive, I don't know if I'd understand it. It's hard to believe."

"You do believe it, though, right? I mean, money's a pretty good motive."

"I'll believe it when the investigation's done and all the evidence is on the table." It still remained to be seen how much money had been gleaned from the murder spree, but it didn't sound life-changing.

"You've got to be kidding me," Riley said. "His hair was practically inside Iris's medicine bottle. Walter's insulin was hidden in his bathroom. And they think that bottle of cleanser with his fingerprints is antifreeze."

"I know, I know," Triss said. After getting a warrant to finish searching the apartment, police had found a generic cleanser bottle filled with what they suspected to be coolant. They were still waiting on results from the food testing to see if any of the meals had been contaminated. "I'm not saying I don't believe it, exactly. I'm just saying it's hard to believe."

She glanced across the room at Courtney, who was helping Iris stick her thankful leaves to the poster tree, and her heart dropped. The defeat and sadness in her eyes were palpable. She must be horrified to know that she'd been so close to a murderer. She and Zach had only been together for a few months, but they'd practically been attached at the hip. She felt sorry for the girl. Setting aside the popcorn strand, she forced herself to stand.

"Want some cocoa?" she asked Courtney. "I'm getting myself a mug."

"Sure."

Triss returned quickly with two steaming mugs, handing one to Courtney. "You doing okay?"

Courtney stared into her mug, her forehead creased in worry lines. "Been better."

Kaye came up beside them and put her arm around the girl's shoulders. "I'm sorry, dear."

"We need some music, and none of this elevator Christmas junk," George announced, drawing all their attention. "Wasn't Zach's family coming to sing for us tonight? Wouldn't let them in if they came here with Santa and his eight reindeer."

Courtney sniffled and turned away from the room, taking her cocoa with her. Triss thought about following, but knew she probably needed a little privacy.

"We could have a sing-along," Triss suggested, not quite sure she was hearing her own voice.

"A sing-along!" Kaye repeated. "That's a fine idea." She yanked the cover off the piano in the corner. "I'm sure there are some old Christmas books in this bench." She lifted the lid and started rifling through the stack of books inside. "Give me five minutes here."

Triss sat and started to pick up her neglected and rather sorry-looking strand of popcorn, but the sound of Levi's little voice grabbed her attention.

"Is it Cwismiss?" he asked with a bright smile as he charged into the room, his feet tumbling so fast in front of him that he tripped again, barely breaking stride before picking himself up and charging directly toward Triss.

She knew she shouldn't pick him up, but she couldn't resist. His wispy dark hair always smelled like strawberries, and his warm little hands always smelled like Oreos. He grasped her into a tight hug and then shoved right off and ran to the thankful tree. "What is it?" he asked curiously.

Kaye's answer was lost to Triss as Hunter walked in behind Josie, both of them toting trays of some goodies.

Josie smiled shyly at Triss. "We made cookies," she said, bringing her tray directly to Triss. "Want one?"

"We were very careful not to use any dairy," Hunter said.

They were a mess—misshaped stockings and googly-eyed angels with far too much frosting and even more sprinkles—but Triss wouldn't think of refusing. She took one and bit heartily into it, complimenting

Josie on the taste and decoration. Josie broke into a big grin, leaned close and whispered, "My cookies are on Dad's tray. These are Levi's."

Hunter held out a much more palatable sampling, and Triss laughed, taking a less gooey Christmas-tree-shaped cookie.

"Nice job," she said, and she meant it. Josie beamed and turned away, offering cookies to others in the room as Hunter did the same.

Triss tried not to stare, but she wanted to commit this night to memory. If she'd learned anything in life, it was that happiness was fleeting and life changed in an instant.

The door alarm beeped and Triss was surprised to see Luke walk in with his wife, Natalie.

Triss crossed the room and hugged them both. "I didn't know you were coming."

"Thought we'd join the festivities, see how you were doing," Luke said, his arm slipping around his wife's waist. Months after their wedding, they still seemed to glow, and Triss could be nothing but happy for them both. She'd begun to think that raising her and Cal had ruined Luke's chances of ever finding love, but then he'd met Natalie and it seemed their story had been written from the beginning of time.

"Welcome," Kaye said, introducing herself and doling out hugs all around. "Make yourself at home. We were about to have a little sing-along." She bustled back to the piano. "I've got a whole pile of music," she announced. "But I'm not a singer. Who's going to lead us?"

Brandon hurried over to the music system and cut

off the recording. Silence fell over the room, no one volunteering.

"Guess we were spoiled with Zach," George mused. "Too bad he was trying to kill us all the while."

For one broken moment, it seemed like everyone's spirits had deflated, the reality of the past weeks setting in hard and cold. Triss ached with the sadness, and without thinking, she stood. "I haven't done much singing in years, but I can handle a few Christmas carols."

She went up to the piano, avoiding Hunter's gaze, and wondered what had even gotten into her. It had been years since she'd felt remotely like celebrating Christmas. Years since she'd felt like she'd truly belonged somewhere.

"What do you think we should start with?" Kaye asked, showing her the table of contents on one of the books.

"Oh, definitely this one," Triss said, and focused on the book in front of her instead of the now-silent friends who all sat watching her expectantly.

Kaye began to play "Have Yourself a Merry Little Christmas," and Triss took a deep breath, then hummed quietly with the introduction, getting herself in tune. Then she began to sing, reunited with the music she'd left behind years ago. She'd sung an entire verse before she realized no one was singing with her, and she finally turned to them, waving for them to sing.

They did so haltingly at first, but then the voices filled the commons, staff pausing and taking seats to join in, and all felt right with the world—if only for a time. She took in the sight of Hunter and his kids, and her heart swelled with the knowledge that this was their farewell night. And then her gaze lit on her brother and his wife. Luke's eyes shone with the light he'd always hung on to, the light she'd always craved. Tonight was time, she thought. Time to tell her brother everything.

Hunter couldn't sing. He was transfixed by Triss's voice. She'd squeezed onto the bench next to Kaye, her legs stretched out to the side and crossed at the ankles. Maybe it was her casual slippers and leggings, or maybe it was the warm, lilting tone of her voice, but she seemed softer somehow. Relaxed in a way he'd never known her to be. He suspected that through finally telling her secret, she had been able to find a measure of peace in sharing the burden she had kept so close to her heart for so long. For that, he was happy for her.

And now that Zach had been arrested, Hunter could transfer back to his former position without any reservations. It was as it should be, he told himself, even as Josie stood and wandered to the piano, playing with Triss's hair as the crowd began to sing "O Holy Night." Triss turned slightly to wink at Josie, and Hunter's heart cracked open a little more at the shy grin on Josie's face.

They could have been good together, the four of them. In a different world, anyway. When Triss had told him about her daughter, he'd had a ray of hope for a few seconds. This was something he assumed they could get through together. But when she confided the depth of heartache she felt every time she allowed herself to get close to his kids, whenever she thought about all she'd missed with her daughter, he'd known.

He would never try to convince her to stay. The cost would be too high. He'd done all the convincing and persuading he'd needed to do to get Viv to marry early and put off school. His selfishness had robbed her of her life. He refused to do the same thing to Triss, knowing that every happy moment would be tainted with sorrow.

She had a plan and she'd worked hard for it. Maybe one day, she would think beyond her career and consider a family. But today wasn't that day, and Hunter's family wasn't that family.

By the time Kaye was running out of Christmas songs, Levi and Josie were running out of steam. Hunter scooped Levi into his arms, where his son promptly settled his head onto Hunter's shoulder and popped a thumb in his mouth.

"It's about that time," he said to Josie, who had curled up on the couch next to George, her cheeks pink from exhaustion. She pushed herself up from the couch and turned to hug George goodbye before walking over to Hunter and grasping his hand.

"Sweet girl," George said to Hunter. "Reminds me of my grandbabies when they were babies." He stood. "I think I'll be getting to bed myself."

Luke and Natalie stood as well, and Triss finished shoving the piano books in the bench. "Me, too, if I'm going to get up and run tomorrow," she said.

Josie pulled her hand away from Hunter's and approached Triss with her arms wide open.

"'Night, Triss," she said, and Triss crouched, wrapping her arms around Hunter's daughter and kissing her on the top of her head.

"Thanks for singing with me tonight," Triss said.

Josie grinned. "I'm singing next week at my school's talent show. Can you come?"

"Oh, I—"

"It's on Friday." She looked up at Hunter. "What time, Daddy?"

"Six. But Triss has a lot going on right now, sweetie," he said, giving Triss the out he knew she was searching for.

Josie's smile fell.

"I would love to, but I work next Friday," Triss said gently. Hunter knew she was telling the truth, but he also knew she could easily switch shifts with someone. "Maybe your dad can record it for me?"

"Sure," Hunter replied.

Josie nodded, a small smile reappearing as she said goodbye to Triss.

Triss walked with the group out of the commons before turning into the hallway that led to her apartment, and all the things Hunter wanted to say seemed poorly timed. Part of him wanted to tell Triss that he could wait for her. That if she ever came to a point in her life where she could consider a family, he'd still be here. But he knew the best thing for her, for his kids, for him even, would be closure. She'd said all she needed to say to him at the creek by the church. He would honor her wishes if it killed him.

"Be safe in the morning," he said as Josie opened the front door and cold air blew in.

Triss nodded, her gaze holding his for a moment too long, as if she wanted to say things, too.

Instead, she leaned forward and kissed Levi's cheek, then held the door open for Hunter as he walked with his kids out into the bitter night. He heard her quietly ask her brother and Natalie to stay for a bit, and his heart constricted, knowing that she'd finally found the courage to tell her story—he hoped that her brother would respond in a way that protected her heart.

He didn't like leaving like this, with so many things left unsaid. He opened the car door for Josie and then buckled Levi into his car seat, then cast his gaze around the dark parking lot and to the lights still glowing from within Creekside Manor. Truth be told, he didn't like leaving Harmony at all.

Yes, Zach had been arrested, but his arrest had been so easy. The guy seemed smart. Why would he keep evidence in his apartment? Was he simply that confident that no one would suspect him? And he'd volunteered for the search. That was nagging at Hunter.

He got in his truck and drove slowly out of the lot, scanning the darkened area and the trees beyond. If he expected to see a looming murderer, he saw nothing of the kind. Only nearly bare trees shivering in the cold night, and one of the new security officers doing a nightly patrol loop in a golf cart. He had no reason for the unease he felt as he drove through the opened wrought-iron gate and turned onto the highway. No reason to worry about Triss or the other residents after tucking his kids into bed and locking the house up.

He still felt uneasy, and he still worried, but he certainly had no reason to set his alarm early enough to keep an eye on Triss on her morning run. Still, he stopped what he was doing and set his alarm.

She'd be mad when she saw him following her, but she'd have to deal with it until Hunter was satisfied with the answers the police were able to extract from Zach.

He climbed into bed and stared into the dark, thinking about the prayer meeting he'd been roped into the previous morning at the hospital. When Roman had shown up and offered to pray with Luke over Triss, Hunter had felt compelled to stay instead of leave, like he normally would. And he'd felt that same stirring he'd felt in the little Harmony chapel on Sunday.

He thought about Josie's sweet smile and Levi's contagious energy for life, and how his wife would have wanted him to keep bringing them to church—not just on the holidays. As he stared into the pitch-black room, he was suddenly overwhelmed by the darkness, and he switched on his bedside lamp. At once, his pulse relaxed and he settled against his pillow, his mind drifting to the sermon on bringing all darkness into the light.

It was painful to acknowledge, but he had not really been living for the past two years. He'd been surviving. Grieving the loss of his wife privately, trying to be two parents to his kids, figuring out how to care for them and support them, provide for them, and work all at the same time. What would it look like to start living again?

Triss's face flashed through his mind, but he didn't allow himself to go down that path. He could start living again as a single dad to two kids. It would begin with somehow accepting the fact that this was his new life.

For better or for worse, he had two amazing kids to love and protect and provide for. It was more than enough.

It would have to be.

He leaned over and double-checked his alarm clock, then closed his eyes, sending up a prayer that God would somehow shine light into this life he was trying to live.

It seemed like only minutes later that his alarm clock woke him up. He got ready quickly and then set off toward Triss's college campus. He'd catch her running on the road. Hopefully, he wouldn't scare her.

But he was just out of his driveway when he realized the truck felt rough on the road. He pulled over to the curb and stepped out, taking a quick walk around the vehicle only to find that the rear passenger tire was flat.

Great.

It wouldn't take long to fix, but it wasn't something he felt like dealing with on a cold fall morning in the dark. He pulled the truck into his driveway so he could get some light going, then grabbed out his jack. It was then that a thought occurred to him.

What were the chances that he would wake up with a flat that would make him late to meet Triss? Alarmed, but figuring he was being overly cautious, he called Triss's cell. When she didn't pick up, he texted her, asking her to call back immediately.

As he waited for her to respond, he yanked out his spare tire and made quick work of the tire change.

She texted him as he finished tightening the bolts.

On my run. Everything okay?

He had brought the flat tire into the garage to inspect, searching for a telltale nail.

He texted his reply.

Planned to keep an eye out for you this morning. Woke up to a flat. What can I do to convince you to head back until I get there?

He didn't see a nail or screw and set down the tire to finish tightening the bolts on the spare and then put the jack away.

Just got to the campus. I'm armed. I'll be fine.

He sighed. Of course she wouldn't agree. And by the time he got to the campus, she'd be nearly done with her workout. He'd go, anyway, maybe have a little conversation with her about waiting to go places alone until they had more answers about the investigation.

He went to the garage to close it up, but felt compelled to look at the tire again. The light in the garage was dim. He grabbed a flashlight out of his toolbox and inspected the tire more carefully. It didn't take him long to find the cause of the flat, and when he did, his blood ran cold. A fine line, maybe two inches long, had been neatly sliced into the rubber along one of the tire grooves. Nearly undetectable. He dialed Triss with one hand as he closed the garage door with the other, and then jumped in his truck. Why wasn't she picking up?

THIRTEEN

Triss's legs were burning, and so were her lungs. The morning was brutally cold, and she'd found herself asking why on earth she felt so compelled to come out here and run the bleachers any day at all, let alone on a frosty fall morning.

But the truth was, her early-morning runs were her way of gathering strength and clearing her mind. As she raced up the bleachers, she thought about Zach and how little she had truly known him. Sure, she had never had any real attachment to him, like she'd developed with some of the residents, but she was still shocked. He'd never seemed like a threat. How had those innocent eyes and smooth voice fooled them all?

But even as she wondered, she was relieved the culprit had been caught. An investigation would certainly happen now, and maybe justice would be served if he'd participated in the deaths of the four deceased residents. She thought back to Iris and the ferry. Had Zach thrown her overboard? He certainly had the strength. But he'd been trying to save her—had alerted everyone and thrown her the life preserver. She frowned, remembering how he'd helped during Triss's allergic reaction. And why target Triss in the first place? Why kill four residents?

The questions would drive her crazy, and she could only hope that the entire truth would eventually be revealed. In the meantime, she was reclaiming her life. Last night she'd finally told Luke about her daughter.

At first, his eyes had looked so stricken that she'd immediately wanted to take it back, keep the secret she'd been living with for far too long. Instead, she'd ventured forth, the story tumbling out like it had earlier with Hunter, only this time, she couldn't read Luke's eyes.

By the time she'd finished, she'd been sure she knew what he was going to say. He was going to ask her why. He was going to wish she'd told him, insist that he would have helped. She braced herself for it.

"I'd always wondered," he had finally said, a sad smile on his face. "Thank you for telling me. I just wish you hadn't gone through all of that alone."

Then he'd said what she'd needed to hear most of all: "You did the right thing, Triss. The hardest thing. The most sacrificial thing. I'm proud of you."

His words brought freedom, and her heart still swelled with the affirmation. He hadn't said what she'd imagined all along he would say.

But then, he'd opened his mouth again. "I have two questions."

Her heart had pitched as she waited for it. Waited for the regret and the "why didn't you?" and the questions.

"What did you name her? And do you think we'll ever get to meet her?"

At the memory, she blinked back tears, heart swelling with the love she'd seen in her brother's eyes. She'd let the adoptive parents name her, but she'd called her Joy for the last two months of her pregnancy, as if speaking the name would somehow make it true for her life.

Her footsteps echoed on the metal steps as she neared the bottom, and when she reached that final step, it was all she could do to motivate herself to circle around and head up for her last rep. The wind blew cold and fierce, and was somehow cleansing. She'd felt lighter ever since she'd told Hunter about her daughter. And even lighter after telling Luke. For all these years, her life had been driven by the secret as she'd thrown herself into her education and career path and shied away from relationships. All to avoid the grief of loss. But now that the secret had finally come to light, she suddenly felt more heavily burdened by the questions she had rarely allowed herself to ask.

Where was her daughter? What was her family like? Was she happy? Healthy? Loved? She'd sent the email to the adoption agency earlier in the week, and its receipt had been acknowledged by a social worker. However, she had yet to hear any news about her daughter.

She pushed through the burning quads and biting wind, nearing the top of the bleachers again, then jumped at the vibration of her phone in her jacket pocket.

Probably Hunter again, she figured. She'd call him after she finished the set, or he'd worry himself into a frenzy and end up driving over here, anyway. Too hard to get her gloves off now, get her phone out of her pocket and answer.

Finally, she reached the top, and considered the idea of laying off the daily bleacher workout for the rest of the winter. The phone stopped vibrating and almost immediately started again.

Thirty seconds and she'd call back.

But even as the thought flitted through her mind, a swift movement from behind made her stumble. She gasped, just as a dark figure came at her, some kind of weapon in hand. Before Triss could react, something heavy slammed into her, and she went flying.

Her feet flew out from under her as she fell forward, missing several steps before smashing into the bleachers.

Instinctively, her arms wrapped around her head, and her forearms were the first part of her body to connect with the metal edge of one of the bleacher steps. Sharp pain shot through her left arm, and she was tumbling forward, unable to stop herself, her body banging against each cold, hard step until she lost momentum and finally came to a rest.

For a moment, she was stunned, pain flaring all over her body. She blinked, disoriented, and managed to roll to her right side, pushing herself up.

Her adrenaline took over and she forced herself to ignore a throbbing ankle as she started to right herself. But footsteps crashed on the bleachers above her and she turned her head in time to see someone she never would have expected to be outside on a frigid morning.

It took her a moment too long to realize that Courtney hadn't come along for an uncharacteristic morning jog. In fact, she only realized it when Courtney got close enough for Triss's running light to pick up the heavy black baton Courtney was wielding.

Desperately, Triss started to roll toward the bottom of the bleachers, her good hand reaching under her jacket to retrieve her gun. Her fingers were clumsy under her thermal gloves, but she had to try. She grabbed at the holster of the gun as Courtney took a well-aimed swing. Triss managed to dodge the hit, but Courtney slashed the baton toward her again, relentless, her face contorted into a murderous rage. Triss's cell phone kept vibrating.

Hunter was afraid of what he'd find when Triss didn't answer his phone calls, but nothing could have prepared him for the sight of her sprawled at the bottom of the bleachers, scrambling for escape.

Her attacker, dressed all in black, hovered over her, a heavy dark stick of some sort poised to strike again as Hunter lunged up the steps to reach her.

"Freeze!" he yelled, gun already in hand.

The dark figure froze, a pale face jerking upward.

Hunter slowed, yards away now, his gun trained on who he now realized, with no small amount of confusion, was Courtney.

"Drop it, Courtney," he commanded, approaching with measured steps. All he wanted to do was run to Triss, call for help, make sure she was okay. But he couldn't risk taking his eyes off of the girl with the wild-looking eyes who held what he now realized was a police baton like a deadly baseball bat, poised at shoulder height.

"Put it down," he repeated.

And, to his surprise, she did. She let the baton drop, and it clattered to the bleachers, where it clanged down several steps before rolling to a stop. He lunged toward her, but she took off, feet flying across metal as she tried to escape. With barely a thought, Hunter holstered his gun and ran after her.

To his surprise, Triss managed to get on her feet and follow her, too. With one swift leap, she brought Courtney down to the cold hard bleachers as Hunter caught up with the two.

Courtney struggled, her harsh breathing the only evidence that she was in any way distressed as Hunter crouched next to her and yanked her hands behind her back, taking over for Triss.

"It's her fault," Courtney growled, her cheek to the ground. "It's all her fault." Her voice was gritty and strange, her eyes staring but not seeing. Hunter glanced toward Triss, saw her fumbling to pull out her phone.

"I called Goodson on my way here," he said, and she let the phone drop, leaning against a bleacher step and holding her arm.

"What did you do, Courtney?" he asked, not expecting an answer. "What did you do?"

"It's all her fault," she repeated, her voice nearly drowned out by the nearing sirens. "None of them were happy. None of them."

A sick feeling washed over Hunter as he held her down, though she wasn't struggling anymore. He exchanged glances with Triss, and she seemed to read his mind, picking up her phone and pressing Record.

"Did you kill them, Courtney?" he asked.

"They wanted to go," she said.

"Did you kill them?" he asked again.

"They wanted to go!" she yelled then, and then she was silent.

Triss scooted closer. "You're right, Courtney," she said, her soft voice surprising even Hunter. "Your grandfather wasn't happy."

"None of them were," Courtney groaned.

"So you gave them an out," Triss said softly. Her tone didn't match the sick realization in her eyes, but Courtney couldn't see that. "Took some of their money for your troubles."

"They wanted me to have the money." Courtney's voice changed from an angry monotone to a strangled wail. "They wanted me to have it! But you couldn't leave us alone. You couldn't understand." She let out a guttural wail of sorrow and rage that echoed through the stadium and sent a chill straight to Hunter's core.

A misguided nurse who doled out mercy killings? Or a greedy graduate student with a penchant for murder? He had a feeling the truth was somewhere in between, trapped in the deranged mind of this young woman none of them had really known.

The sirens were close now, as law enforcement vehicles soon arrived on the street behind the stadium, and Hunter's pulse started to slow. They hadn't been able to save the four victims, but they'd managed to stop Courtney from succeeding a fifth time. Now, there would be justice, and he could rest knowing that Triss was safe. His gaze settled on her face, pale as the sun that began to rise behind the bleachers. Soon it would be time to say goodbye, but he still wished he didn't have to.

FOURTEEN

Triss was tired. But not the sleepy kind of tired. She was the kind of tired that happens after living six years in survival mode. The kind of tired that happens after surviving several near-death experiences. The kind of tired that happens when fighting against all she'd ever wanted led her to a place where she had started to wonder why she'd ever fought it at all. And then discovered it was too late.

She sighed, thinking about the weeks and months ahead. She'd need to request exemptions for her classes and take the rest of the semester off. Surprisingly, she wasn't all that disappointed.

The idea of rest, mental and physical, for the first time in her life, actually sounded somewhat appealing to her. She'd have to find something to do with her time, though, because she'd spent far too much time checking her phone this week—for a text from Hunter, a call from Officer Goodson or a message from the adoption agency. She'd drive herself crazy doing this for weeks.

It was Friday now, and already she wished she could

go back to school and work. She'd managed to escape Courtney's attack with only a sprained ankle, a fractured arm and a minor concussion, and Roman had rewarded her survival with five weeks of paid vacation to finish out her Shield career. He'd jokingly explained that he didn't think her brother or Hunter would be able to handle another hospital stay of hers. Still recovering, she wasn't supposed to spend time in front of screens or do anything remotely taxing, even reading. That had left far too much time to think. The doctors had warned her that the more she rested, the faster she'd get better. So, she'd rested.

Except that she hadn't rested in years, so her version of resting entailed entirely too much thinking and processing.

Courtney had confessed to the four murders in exchange for a plea deal that could allow for parole in thirty-five years, though she would be unlikely to be granted it. As suspected, she'd used her grandfather's insulin while he slept to put him into a diabetic coma. She'd gotten more creative with the others. She'd injected bleach into Genevieve's dialysis line, causing the fatal heart attack. Simple suffocation with a pillow for Connie Mays, and dissolved painkillers in Frank Townsend's beer.

Strangely, she hadn't taken that much money from any of the victims—maybe because she was afraid she'd get caught. She used disguises at the ATMs and "borrowed" residents' cars late at night. As for targeting Triss, it seemed that Triss had become a threat, limiting Courtney's ability to follow through with the mercy killings she'd felt she was called to perform. Triss shuddered at the thought.

The final question was how the evidence showed up in Zach's apartment, and whether he'd been her accomplice.

Courtney claimed that she'd just stored the supplies there—easier access because her apartment was in a far corner. Triss found that hard to believe, but trusted that the truth would unfold with time.

Now it was Friday afternoon, and she was thinking that her head wasn't hurting as bad, and one episode of a new show on Netflix couldn't possibly do any more damage. She'd watch it with only a small amount of guilt, help herself to some hot cocoa from the kitchen and curl up on the comfy new bedding Kaye had bought for her.

With no small amount of effort, she climbed into bed, turned on her television and set her phone next to her.

She'd done a good job not thinking much about the adoption agency or Hunter in the past couple of days. There'd been a lot going on with the investigation into Courtney that had occupied her attention.

The show came on, and she settled against the pile of pillows she'd made for herself, determined not to check her phone again, but within minutes, it dinged, and she glanced over to see an email notification.

Her heart nearly fell out of her chest when she saw the name of the adoption agency pop up.

She sat up quickly—too quickly. The room shifted around her as she turned off the TV and picked up her phone.

Her hand shook as she swiped up to unlock the phone, then clicked on the email.

Joy.

She gasped, tears springing from her eyes at the image on her screen.

Her daughter, without a doubt. Dark, joyful eyes set against a cherubic butterscotch face, bouncy curls in disarray. Her smile was wide and uninhibited, and two front teeth were proudly missing.

She stared long enough for the screen to time out, and she swiped at it again, taking in the sight of the daughter she had carried for nine months and held for two days. The daughter she had sung to and read to in utero on long lonely nights in the teen crisis center, had desperately prayed for even after she'd stopped believing God would answer her prayers. The daughter whose life had driven every moment for Triss over the past several years, even if she had convinced herself she had learned to move on.

Triss set the phone on the bed and swiped the mess of tears away from her eyes, then scrolled further in the email. She read a short note from the social worker, announcing that the adoptive family had been contacted—and that they welcomed the idea of connecting with Triss.

Her heart pounded as she clicked on the message the adoptive parents had given the social worker to send to her, and then the message opened and she began to read.

We have prayed this day would come since the moment Joy was placed in our arms. Yes, we kept her name—

you chose it perfectly, and you can see from the expression on her face that she lives it out.

Triss didn't realize she was sobbing until her eyes
were so filled with tears that she could no longer read
the letter. She dropped the phone onto her lap and gave
in to the tears, the relief so palpable she had never felt
such joy. Seeing her daughter, hearing about her life,
being affirmed that she was not only okay, but also
thriving—somehow it all gave Triss *new* life. New hope.

She pulled herself together and kept reading, about
Joy's two younger siblings and the family's life. Their
family nights and camping trips, Joy's affinity for singing and her ability to see the best in everyone. It reminded Triss of herself—how she might have been as
a child if the world hadn't shown its ugly side. By the
time she had finished reading, she knew two things and
two things only: first, yes, she was going to meet her
daughter next Sunday like the family had offered. And
second, she absolutely needed to see Hunter.

She looked at the clock and started to call him but
suddenly realized what day it was. Friday. Five past six.
Josie's talent show.

She pushed herself off the bed, limping on her bad
ankle, and shoved her feet into a pair of slipper boots.
She didn't even spare a glance in the mirror, but grabbed
her purse and hurried out of her apartment.

Kaye was the first person she found, and the woman
looked up from her book, surprised.

"Doctor says no driving," she said, eyeing Triss's
purse.

"I'm not," Triss said, unable to contain her smile. "You are. Want to take me to Josie's talent show? I'm already late."

Kaye jumped up so fast that Iris woke up next to her. "Just let me grab my keys! Come on, Iris, we have a show to watch."

"Whose talent show is this again?" Iris asked several minutes later from the back seat as she snapped her seat belt.

"Little Josie's." Kaye reversed too quickly out of her parking spot, then slammed on the gas down the yards of gravel to the wrought-iron gate.

Triss laughed, grabbing the side pocket of the door for equilibrium.

"Oh, that sweet girl," Iris said with delight.

The gate slid open in slow motion and Kaye glanced over at Triss, her gaze flicking from her eyes to her hair and to her red leggings and black slippers.

"There's a comb in my purse," she said.

"A comb won't hold up to this mess," Triss said, absently flipping down the sun visor and peeking in the mirror. "Oh, wow." Maybe she should have taken those extra minutes to pull herself together after all.

"Try the comb, dear," Kaye insisted.

Iris passed Kaye's purse up, and Triss reached inside, pulling out a thin black comb with fine bristles. It was a sweet gesture, but the comb would break in her hair on the first pass-through.

"It won't work, but thanks for trying." Instead, she worked her fingers through her hair by sections, loosening the tangles and taming the mess. She rummaged around in her purse and managed to locate a rubber band, which she used to pull her hair into a low ponytail. She looked at Kaye at the next red light. "Better?"

Kaye sighed, but a soft smile formed. "Much. Anyhow, I doubt the love of your life would walk away because your hair's a fright and you're wearing your pajamas to his daughter's school talent show."

"The love of her life?" Iris asked, leaning forward.

"Josie and Levi's handsome father, Iris," Kaye said with good-natured annoyance. "When will you get your new prescription? You're missing all the important stuff."

Triss broke into real laughter at Kaye's words, her heart lighter than it had been for as long as she could remember. She had no interest in denying it. Hunter was, absolutely, the love of her life. But then, her smile fell. He might not be up to giving her another chance. She'd walked away twice, and he had no reason to believe that she could be trusted.

The school was just around the next corner, and her heart sped up. She glanced at her leggings and wished she'd changed. "For the record, this isn't pajamas," she said, attempting humor even as nerves took hold.

Kaye shrugged. "You've been wearing them for two straight days. I'm guessing you've been sleeping in them."

Triss couldn't disagree.

"Like I said, pajamas. But I doubt Hunter will mind."

"These aren't slippers, either," Triss said. "They're slipper-like boots."

Kaye laughed at that and pulled into the packed school parking lot. "Okay."

Kaye found a parking space and the three women climbed out of the car. It was sunny and cold, and the school was silent. Triss paused and looked at her watch, immediately questioning her spontaneous decision.

"What's the matter?" Kaye asked.

"Maybe I should wait in the car until it's over," Triss said. "We're late. For all I know, I've already missed Josie. And I don't want to make a scene and—"

Kaye marched over and linked her arm through Triss's good arm. "We're here. We're going in. Maybe you're not too late. If you are, at least you tried."

Reluctantly, Triss let Kaye lead her toward the school, Iris flanking her other side. Triss imagined that this might have been what it would have felt like to have a mother, and she felt the years of experience Kaye had with her many daughters. Somehow, that was comforting, and she knew that no matter what happened, she wouldn't be alone.

The warmth inside the building wasn't enough to cut the sudden chill Triss felt, but she kept moving toward the auditorium, anyway. The sounds of laughter beckoned their little group, and together they slipped into the darkened auditorium as an adorable nine-year-old finished up a series of surprisingly funny knock-knock jokes.

"Sorry, we're out of programs," a greeter whispered to Triss, as she followed Kaye to a set of three seats nearby. There was nothing open closer to the stage, which was just as well. The auditorium was not that big, and they could see the stage fine.

Kaye and Iris filed into the seats and Triss took the aisle seat, her heart rate settling as a trio of little boys set up their drums and began a fun take on "The Little Drummer Boy."

Triss peered out over the audience, unable to find Hunter and Levi in the shadows. As more acts went onstage and the hour grew late, she realized she must have missed Josie after all. Disappointment mixed with second-guessing her decision to come in the first place.

"Maybe we should go," she whispered to Kaye.

Kaye glanced her way. "Let's see it through."

Triss was about to insist, knew that Kaye would agree if she pushed, but then Josie's name was called, and their attention fixed on the stage as Josie took her place on the center X and the spotlight illuminated her.

She stood statue-still and unsmiling, her glittery red tutu-like skirt shimmering under the stage lights as the opening bars of "Have Yourself a Merry Little Christmas" played.

For what felt like minutes, but was only long, terrifying seconds, Josie stood silently, missing her cue. The audience sat silently, too, collectively holding their breath as the little girl stood voiceless.

"Oh, no," Kaye whispered.

Josie's lips quivered, and Triss's heart broke. Without thinking, she jumped out of her seat and jogged down the side aisle, ignoring her tender ankle and slowing down only as she made her way up the steps to the stage so she wouldn't scare Josie.

"Sorry I'm late," Triss whispered as Josie turned to her, her eyes lighting in surprise. "Want a partner?"

FIFTEEN

Josie nodded, her nose pink and eyes wet from the effort not to break down in tears in front of her audience of peers.

Triss offered her hand and turned to the microphone as someone with good sense in the sound room restarted the track.

"I was late for our duet," Triss explained with a smile into the microphone, her heart hammering at the realization of what she'd just done.

A few people chuckled and Josie looked up at Triss as if she was her forever hero. And then their cue came, and Triss started the song, hoping Josie would find her voice.

She did. Within seconds, her voice joined Triss's, and they took turns seamlessly at first, until Triss felt she could let Josie take over the verses. Her entire focus was on Josie, so much so that she couldn't even bring herself to look out into the audience until the final chorus, when Josie reached up for the hand that she'd let go of and they finished the song together.

Hunter's gaze met hers, and Triss nearly lost her breath at the broad smile on his face, the sheer love in his expression. She had a feeling that stepping onstage had told Hunter all he needed to know about her commitment to him and his family. They finished their song and bowed together, walking off the stage to a standing ovation.

Triss squeezed Josie's hand and led her to the row where Hunter was waiting with Levi and Samantha. Hunter motioned for her to wait, whispering something to Samantha. Then he hugged Josie and scooted down the row to the aisle, his hand guiding Triss up the dark aisle to the exit.

Kaye caught Triss's eye as they passed, and she raised knowing eyebrows that made Triss feel like laughing again.

But Hunter reached for the door and they were suddenly out in the silent lobby together, his hand dropping from her as he turned to face her. His expression was serious suddenly, and for an uncertain moment, Triss was afraid he was about to remind her of their agreement.

"I don't think Josie will forget this day for as long as she lives," he said, and his eyes glistened with emotion. "Thank you."

Triss smiled, trying to catch her breath and form her thoughts. She'd rushed away from Harmony and to the school so fast that she hadn't had time to think through what she wanted to say. "I couldn't leave her up there alone," she said. "But I'm sorry I didn't dress for the occasion."

Hunter grinned, his dimples showing. "If you were

going to wear pajamas, at least you chose Christmas pajamas."

Triss's cheeks warmed. "Technically, they're not pajamas."

"You were beautiful up there," he said before she could say anything else, and her heart stopped before it remembered to start beating again. Hunter shoved his hands in the pockets of his black slacks, and for the first time Triss's attention hit on his tie.

Her lips twitched at the Charlie Brown cartoons adorning the busy tie he'd paired with a wintry blue dress shirt. "You're not so bad yourself with that amazing tie."

He rocked on his heels. "It was this one or the one with blinking Christmas lights. Josie bought them for me at her school's Christmas fair yesterday and gave them to me today so I'd have something festive to wear."

"She's something," Triss said, not sure how to transition to what she wanted to say, not sure if the time was right, or the place.

"I didn't expect you to be here," Hunter said after a short pause. The humor was gone now, and he searched her eyes expectantly, as if he knew something had changed.

"I hadn't planned to come." The auditorium erupted suddenly with cheers and applause and the doors opened.

"Looks like the show's over," Hunter said.

Triss fought disappointment and relief as people started to filter out. They'd run out of time, but she had so much still to say.

"Daddy!" Levi practically flew out of the auditorium and launched himself into Hunter's arms. Hunter didn't miss a beat, scooping him up and shifting him easily to one arm as Samantha and Josie caught up.

Josie walked straight up to Triss and wrapped her arms around her waist. Triss crouched and rubbed her back, wishing she could pick her up, but was hindered by the bulky cast on her left arm. "You were so brave up there," she whispered in her ear.

"Only after you came," Josie said, not yet looking up.

"Are you kidding me? At your age, I wouldn't have gone onstage to try to sing even if someone had paid me a million dollars."

Josie giggled and pulled back to look into Triss's face. "I'm glad you came," she said with a happy smile, her cheeks pink.

"Me, too."

Triss stood and realized that Josie had slipped her little hand into hers. She caught Samantha's observant gaze as it moved from Triss and Josie to Hunter and Levi.

"Can we get hot chocolate?" Josie asked, pointing to the tables of refreshments.

"How about we fill up our cups and walk the long way home to look at Christmas lights and stop by the playground?" Samantha asked, looking to Hunter for agreement. "You could go home ahead of us and start the popcorn for the movie."

Josie and Levi were already running to the hot-cocoa dispensers, and Triss could have hugged Samantha for her intuition.

"Sounds like a plan," Hunter said. "Thanks." He turned to Triss, a question in his eyes. "In the mood for popcorn and a Christmas movie with my crew?"

She nodded, her heart full. "Let me tell Kaye and Iris."

The drive to his house would be short, but they would have time to talk before Samantha and the kids got home.

Kaye hugged her, careful of her cast. "Just call me if you need a ride," she said, and then looked straight into her eyes. "Whatever you do, leave nothing unsaid and you'll have no regrets."

Triss tucked away the advice as Hunter walked up to the three of them. He greeted both women with hugs and assured them he would make sure Triss got home safely tonight, and together they made their way through the crowded lobby out into the now-dark evening.

Christmas was in the air, and so was new hope, and Triss's stomach fluttered with anticipation as Hunter walked her to the passenger side of his truck and leaned forward to open the door for her.

But then he paused, his hand on the handle, and she turned to face him.

"Tell me I'm not reading into this," he said, his voice thick with emotion. "I feel like something's changed, but…"

"*Everything* has changed," Triss said, the words coming out in a whisper of breath that charged the air between them with all that they'd been fighting against and hoping for.

Without a second's thought, she stepped close and

pressed a kiss to his lips, the chill in the air disappearing in the span of a single heartbeat.

Hunter's hand slipped from the door and wrapped around her waist. He tugged her closer, his warmth enveloping her for just seconds until he reluctantly pulled away and opened the door for her.

She was barely thinking straight when she got into the truck, still reaching for what to say, how to explain.

Hunter drove carefully through the lot, which was filled with kids and families heading home. The radio station was playing Christmas music, and neighborhood homes were already lit up with decorations. They rode in companionable silence for the three minutes it took to get to his house. He seemed to know that whatever Triss had to say couldn't be said in the span of the short car trip.

But as he pulled into his driveway, Triss was overwhelmed with the realization that if she followed through, her entire life was about to change. Doubt nagged at her mind. Had she reacted out of emotion? She'd been through a lot of trauma. Maybe she should have taken more time to think about the future before she'd run off to see Hunter.

How could she be part of Hunter's life—of his kids' lives—and pursue a career that could move her away?

Hunter came around to her side and opened the truck, offering a hand as she stepped down, and then he didn't let go of her hand as they walked and he opened the front door for her.

The scent of cinnamon hit her first, and then she took in the lively scene in front of her—toys on the floor, a Christmas tree half-erected, boxes of decorations in the front room.

Hunter flipped on lights. "Watch your step. It's a mess in here."

It *was* a mess. And it felt like home.

Her questions drifted away, her anxiety dissolved. Fear wouldn't hold her back again. If God could answer her broken prayers, if He could redeem her broken life with a photo and a one-page letter, she knew He could handle her career. Hunter and the kids came first. The rest would work itself out.

Triss followed him to the kitchen, where he pulled out a jar of popcorn and a couple of large bowls, then a lighter. "Good night for a fire," he said, and she followed him into the living room.

He turned on the gas to the fireplace and used the lighter to start the fire. The coffee table was stacked with picture books, several throw blankets in disarray on the couches, pillows and toys decorating the floor.

Triss stood uncertain, wondering if she should start the popcorn or take a seat.

Hunter motioned to the couch. "I think Samantha and the kids will be a while."

She sat, propping her casted arm on the side of the couch, and Hunter took the seat next to her, only inches separating them.

Her heart beat frantically as she gathered the courage to say all that she wanted to say to him. But when she looked into his eyes, she couldn't find the words. How could she explain the change of heart? How could she tell him what she'd realized when she'd looked at

the face of her smiling daughter and read the reassuring letter of her adoptive parents?

He waited silently, and she knew he wouldn't push
her, so she did the only thing she could think of. She
dug her phone out of her pocket and pulled up the photo,
turning the screen so he could see it.

He leaned close, peering at the photo, his shoulder
touching hers.

"Your daughter," he said without her prompting.
"She looks just like you."

His voice warmed her like the soft flames in the fireplace, and she nodded, finally finding her voice again.
"They sent me the picture today. A letter, too. They
want to meet me next Sunday."

His gaze lifted from the photo and settled on her.
"Will you?"

She wasn't able to contain the smile. "I've spent almost six years imagining the worst scenarios, certain
I made the wrong decision. When I finally decided to
face those fears, this is the gift I got. I don't want to
live in fear anymore."

Hunter listened to Triss's words, watched the light
in her eyes, glanced at the face of her daughter, and he
knew. This photo, the message she'd received from the
family, was the first step in healing. It was the break
she'd needed to relieve her of the guilt she'd been carrying for years. It meant freedom from the grief that
had been following her all this time. But he still wasn't
exactly sure what that meant for him and his kids.

As she read him the contents of the letter, her hand

trembled a little holding the phone, and he reached over and placed his hand under hers to steady her grip. There was no doubt that something had shifted between them, but he needed her to say that explicitly. He would not be the one to push her into a relationship she wasn't ready for.

When she finally finished reading, she set her phone in her lap and turned to look at him directly. "Something happened when I saw her face, Hunter," she said, the look in her eyes honest and full of newfound hope. "And when I read that letter. There's no other way to explain it except for this feeling of…forgiveness. Forgiveness, and…freedom. All this grief I've been holding on to was replaced with relief and the assurance that she's where she needs to be. I had to show you myself. Tell you myself."

He waited, still not hearing what he had been hoping for, but unwilling to fish for what might not be there yet for her.

But then she shifted to turn more fully to him, her eyes dark with emotion, a shadow of uncertainty passing through her expression.

"I don't deserve another chance to make things work with you and your kids, Hunter, but I know I'll regret not telling you everything."

"There's more?" he asked, his heart sinking as he began to wonder if he'd again allowed himself to be reeled into hoping for something that wasn't meant to be.

She nodded, her eyes glimmering, the firelight flickering shadows across her face. It took all his willpower to keep from pulling her into his arms and telling her he didn't care what else there was, asking her to simply take a chance on a life together, no matter what was in the past.

But whatever this was, it was obvious that she needed to say it, so he waited.

And then she reached over and intertwined her hand with his. "I love you."

The words, quiet but sure, struck his heart like a swift jolt of electricity, and it took him a second to register their meaning. That was the rest of what she needed to tell him. That was everything. She loved him.

He looked at their hands together, then up into dark eyes full of a hope he'd never seen in Triss before. He didn't trust his voice to tell her all that he wanted to say, but he managed a grin and finally said, "You've probably guessed that the feeling is mutual, but just in case..." He leaned close, sliding a hand along her nape, drawing her toward him. It was a kiss that promised forever, her palm resting just above his heart, and he didn't want it to end. But he heard giggling and footsteps approaching the house, knew Samantha and the kids had arrived, and their time was short. He pulled back from the kiss and cupped the side of Triss's face.

"I love you, too," he said, and she smiled as the door flew open and the kids burst into the house, full of laughter as Samantha followed behind.

Levi launched himself into the living room, smiling broadly under a faint hot-chocolate mustache. "Can we have popcorn now?" he asked, his eyes brighter and more energetic than they should be at such a late hour for a two-year-old.

"Oh, yeah, I forgot about the popcorn," Hunter said, pushing himself up a bit reluctantly.

"I'll help," Triss said, following him to the kitchen.

"Want me to get the kids ready for bed before I head out?" Samantha asked, and Hunter remembered belatedly that she had been planning to go out for a friend's birthday dinner.

"No, you go on ahead," he told her. "I've got it from here."

She hugged the kids goodbye and headed out, and the kids commenced to turn Christmas music on too loud and dance in singing circles in the living room. While Hunter made popcorn, Triss got bowls out and then insisted that Levi get his face cleaned up. He attempted singing and twirling while she wiped off the sticky hot-cocoa residue, and then he danced into the living room.

Hunter turned to offer Triss a bowl of popcorn, but hesitated when he caught her watching the kids. For a moment, he wondered if she was having second thoughts. If this was one of those moments she'd told him about—when what should be happy was filled, instead, with sadness.

"Popcorn?" he asked finally, and she turned to him, amusement in her expression with no hint of the sadness he had imagined.

"Maybe later," she said. "What movie?"

"Frosty the Snowman!" Josie announced.

"No, Gwinch!" Levi yelled.

"Frosty!" Josie yelled louder, her smile falling.

"Gwinch!" Levi yelled back, his voice matching hers in intensity.

"Oh, boy," Triss said.

"You sure you want to sign up for this chaos?" Hunter asked, and even though he was partly joking, he couldn't help but wonder if she really knew what she was getting into.

She turned to him, looked him directly in the eyes and said, "I've never been more certain of anything in my life. Bring on the chaos. I'm ready to live again."

She took the bowl of popcorn from him, brushed a quick kiss to his lips and entered the living-room fight.

"Aren't both of those movies pretty short?" she asked, and the kids stopped and stared at her.

"I'm just saying…maybe we could watch both?"

She sat on the couch and the kids climbed up on either side of her, shoving hands in the popcorn bowl.

"They're pretty short, but it's also pretty late," Hunter said, regretting being the bearer of bad news. "And we'll need to drive Triss home afterward."

"You're staying for the movie?" Josie asked, her voice hopeful.

Triss nodded. "But only if you two stop fighting."

"If you're staying for the movie, I don't care what we watch," Josie said softly, and settled in close to Triss, leaning her head against Triss's arm.

Hunter smiled, his heart tender at the sight. Levi raced over to the television and expertly yanked out the disc to *How the Grinch Stole Christmas*, and Hunter went to the kitchen to flick off the lights for movie night ambience. He settled on the other side of Josie as

Levi shoved the disc into the DVD player and brought Hunter the remote. It was dark, the only lights from the flickering fire and the television screen. But, somehow, the house didn't feel dark at all. For the first time since Vivian's death, Hunter felt the shadows start to lift, new hope flooding in and drowning out the darkness.

As the movie began, he glanced over at Triss, flanked by his two children, and he knew, somehow, that they'd both been given the gift of a new beginning.

* * * * *

Dear Reader,

In real life, I don't have much in common with Triss or Hunter, yet their hearts spoke to mine. In the shadows of their lives, I saw the shadows of my own—the weight of heartbreak, fear, regret and loss, and the yearning to fully live and fully love, despite it all. What Triss and Hunter found to be true in their pursuit of new beginnings, I've also found to be true: we long for a peace that the world can never give us. May you seek and find peace through the power of the Holy Spirit, the gift of His living and breathing Word and the blessing of companionship with loved ones who lift spirits, lighten burdens and offer chocolate.

Love,
Sara

P.S. I love to hear from readers—find me on Facebook @sarakparker.author and on my web site: www.sarakparker.com.

SPECIAL EXCERPT FROM

Love Inspired.
SUSPENSE

*When a guide dog trainer becomes a target
of a dangerous crime ring, a K-9 cop and his loyal
partner will work together to keep her safe.*

Read on for a sneak preview of Trail of Danger
*by Valerie Hansen, the next exciting installment
to the* True Blue K-9 Unit *miniseries,
available September 2019 from Love Inspired Suspense.*

Abigail Jones stared at the blackening eastern sky and shivered. She was more afraid of the strangers lingering in the shadows along the Coney Island boardwalk than she was of the summer storm brewing over the Atlantic.

Early September humidity made the salty oceanic atmosphere feel sticky while the wind whipped loose tendrils of Abigail's long red hair. If sixteen-year-old Kiera Underhill hadn't insisted where and when their secret meeting must take place, Abigail would have stopped to speak with some of the other teens she was passing. Instead, she made a beeline for the spot where their favorite little hot dog wagon spent its days.

Besides the groups of partying youth, she skirted dog walkers, couples strolling hand in hand and an old woman leaning on a cane. Then there was a tall man and enormous dog ambling toward her. As they passed beneath an overhead vapor light, she recognized his police uniform and breathed a sigh of relief. Most K-9 patrols in her nearby neighborhood used German shepherds, so seeing the long floppy ears and droopy jowls of a bloodhound brought a smile despite her uneasiness.

Pausing, Abigail rested her back against the fence surrounding a currently closed amusement park, faced into the wind and waited for the K-9 cop to go by. His unexpected presence could be what was delaying Kiera.

"Come on, Kiera. I came alone, just like you wanted," Abigail muttered.

Kiera had sounded panicky when she'd phoned.

"Here. Over here" drifted on the wind. Abigail strained to listen.

The summons seemed to be coming from inside the Luna Park perimeter fence. That was not good since the amusement facility was currently closed. Nevertheless, she cupped her hands around her eyes and peered through the chain-link fence. It was several seconds before she realized the gate was ajar. *Uh-oh. Bad sign.* "Kiera? Is that you?"

A disembodied voice answered faintly. "Help me! Hurry."

Don't miss
Trail of Danger *by Valerie Hansen,*
available September 2019 wherever
Love Inspired® Suspense *books and ebooks are sold.*

www.LoveInspired.com

Looking for inspiration in tales
of hope, faith and heartfelt romance?

Check out **Love Inspired**® and
Love Inspired® **Suspense** books!

New books available every month!

CONNECT WITH US AT:

Facebook.com/groups/HarlequinConnection

Facebook.com/HarlequinBooks

Twitter.com/HarlequinBooks

Instagram.com/HarlequinBooks

Pinterest.com/HarlequinBooks

ReaderService.com